W9-CTJ-948

"Listen To Me.
The Price Is Too High."

"The price," Mattie whispered, "is worth it."

"Mattie, haven't you heard a word I've been saying? I'm eight years older than you."

"So old, Jace," she mocked.

"Damn it, yes. I've got one failed marriage behind me and a body that could quit any second. I don't need involvement. Not with someone like you, someone who believes in permanence, someone who still has stars in her eyes."

"Do you hear me talking about permanence?"

"You're not the type for an affair," Jace said flatly.

"How do you know?" she murmured. "You got burned once, and you're terrified to risk anything ever again. Isn't that it, Jace?"

She saw the flash of anger in his eyes.

"Mattie, I've got nothing to give."

"Only yourself," she whispered. "Is that nothing?"

Dear Reader:

It's summertime, and I hope you've had a chance to relax and enjoy the season. Here to help you is a new man—Mr. August. Meet Joyce Thies's *Mountain Man*. He thinks he's conquered it all by facing Alaska, America's last frontier...but he hasn't met his mail-order bride yet!

Next month will bring a special man from Dixie Browning. Mr. September—Clement Cornelius Barto—is an unusual hero at best, but make no mistake, it's not just *Beginner's Luck* that makes him such a winner.

I hope you've been enjoying our "Year of the Man." From January to December, 1989 is a twelve-month extravaganza at Silhouette Desire. We're spotlighting one book each month with special cover treatment as a tribute to the Silhouette Desire hero—our *Man of the Month*!

Created by your favorite authors, these men are utterly irresistible. Don't let them get away!

Yours,

Isabel Swift
Senior Editor & Editorial Coordinator

JO ANDREWS
Gale Force

Silhouette Desire

Published by Silhouette Books New York

America's Publisher of Contemporary Romance

SILHOUETTE BOOKS
300 East 42nd St., New York, N.Y. 10017

Copyright © 1989 by Jo Andrews

All rights reserved. Except for use in any review,
the reproduction or utilization of this work in
whole or in part in any form by any electronic,
mechanical or other means, now known or
hereafter invented, including xerography,
photocopying and recording, or in any information
storage or retrieval system, is forbidden without
the permission of Silhouette Books, 300 E. 42nd St.,
New York, N.Y. 10017

ISBN: 0-373-05514-5

First Silhouette Books printing August 1989

All the characters in this book are fictitious. Any
resemblance to actual persons, living or dead, is
purely coincidental.

®: Trademark used under license and
registered in the United States Patent and
Trademark Office and in other countries.

Printed in the U.S.A.

JO ANDREWS

says, "I'm a hopeless romantic. Back as far as I can remember I would create romantic scenarios around the lives of friends or of perfect strangers I'd see on the street, or restructure the plots of movies and books to fit my view of the *vie en rose*. I've always loved exploring human conflicts and problems through the romantic relationships of men and women.

"I live with two travel-weary cats and a travel-mad free-lance photographer. Our trips across North America for business or pleasure give me wonderful opportunities to search out modern-day Edens in which to set my books. Home base at present is Toronto, but that could be subject to change."

One

―――

"Jace Wyatt? Who the hell's this Jason Wyatt?" Bob growled, irritated at being dragged away from the depth sounder he was taking apart. "Can't we talk about it later, Gramps?"

"He's the guy who's gonna save our a—" Gramps caught sight of Mattie curled up on a cushion just outside the deckhouse, a pale glimmer in the velvet-dark softness of the Florida night, and backtracked hastily "—skins."

Mattie laughed. Bob grinned at her. They both knew that Mattie could cuss like a longshoreman when so moved.

"I'm not listening," she said drowsily.

She wasn't. She was leaning back on the gunwhale, half-asleep, contentedly tired after the long day, hearing the mutter of their conversation not so much as words but as sensation.

There was only the murmur of their voices, the lap of the sea against the boat, the creak and shift of the rigging. No other sounds disturbed the depthless, enfolding, somehow intensely alive silence of the night. The sky was brilliant with stars, the Gulf of Mexico was an expanse of fathomless but not empty blackness, and a breeze came from sky and sea, salt scented and cool.

The sense of space and isolation was so deep she felt that they were the only living things on earth—a feeling not of loneliness but of contented solitude. She rested within it, wanting the moment to last forever.

"Wake up, Mattie," said Gramps. "I want you to hear this."

"So how's he going to save our...skins?" asked Bob with a slanted grin at Mattie. His attention was really on the depth sounder and that mad-inventor gleam was back in his eyes.

"Take your squirrelly mind off that and listen to me, you idiot," Gramps snapped. "Can't you hear what I'm saying? I've got backing for that fool flotation device of yours."

"What?" Bob's head jerked up, his eyes incandescent in the bright light of the deckhouse and the spiky strands of his blond, salt-sticky hair almost standing on end.

"Thought that would get to you," Gramps said with satisfaction. He turned and yelled aft. "Sam, yo, Sam! Come up here a minute. You'll want to hear this."

"Right here, Gramps."

Sam Davis came up, cat-soft and silent, on Mattie's left. She smiled at him as he squatted down on his heels beside her, his big hands automatically reaching to neaten a tangle of line.

"What's going on, Mattie?" he asked in his slow, deep voice.

"Gramps," she said simply and he chuckled, almost invisible in the darkness, the brown-black of his skin blending into the blue-black of the night so that all she could see was a solid reassuring bulk beside her and the odd reflection of light from the deckhouse defining forehead or cheek.

"Look," said Gramps, talking more to Bob than to Mattie and Sam. "This business of ours is okay. Between the salvage and the charters, we're breaking even, got food on the table and a roof over our heads. But we could do a lot better if we got that invention of yours going, Bob."

"Damn right," said Bob with flat conviction.

"Only we ain't got the cash to finance it. There's a heap of things you need, boy, before you can even test that gadget of yours and we're mortgaged to the hilt as is. What we need is someone to invest some capital in us."

"And that's this Jace Wyatt," Bob said slowly.

"Right. He gives us the capital and we give him fifty percent of the business."

Mattie sat up. Gramps noted the movement, but did not look around. He waited for Bob to speak. Bob was silent.

"Who would be running things around here?" Mattie asked softly.

Gramps hunched his shoulders uncomfortably. "Anybody. Everybody. The way we do now. Nothing's going to change, Mattie."

"Are you going to guarantee that?"

He looked out of the deckhouse at her. "Mattie, you got to admit neither Bob nor me is any good at organization. Bob's got his mind on his crazy inventions half the time. Me, all I want is the boats, got no liking for the paperwork.''

Mattie did not need to be told that. It was she who kept supplies from running out, placed the orders, paid the invoices, kept the books, took care of the thousand and one things involved in running any business.

''Jace, now,'' said Gramps. ''Jace knows how to run things.''

''Just who is this Jace Wyatt?'' Mattie asked, her voice dead level.

Gramps's face lit up.

''He's an old buddy of mine from when I was in the navy,'' he said and Mattie heard the note of deep affection in his voice. ''He was just a kid when I first met him but he's come a long way in the past fourteen years. He'd made head of the underwater demolition team before I retired. Since then he's become master-at-arms, chief of the boat on the submarine *Hunter*. Braid on his sleeve now. And he's earned it.''

''Career navy? An officer? Then why is he leaving now?''

''He's being invalided out. They had a medical team on board doing deep-pressure research, testing compression effects at varying depths. Charge detonated when it shouldn't. Small charge sets off a mild explosion at thirty fathoms, but it's a rock crusher at three hundred. Jace got hit.''

''Cripple's no use to us,'' Bob said with that innocent callousness that was never meant as it sounded, but came instead from his tunnel vision.

''Hell, he ain't no cripple!'' Gramps roared, his neat white beard bristling. ''He's in fine shape!''

''Then why's he out?''

"He's carrying a piece of iron in his back the doctors can't get out because it's too close to his spine. Certain kind of pressure, exertion, might cause it to slip. Navy can't risk something like that, so he's out, fit or no."

"And here," Mattie murmured.

"And here," Gramps agreed. "Iffen he hadn't a dime, he'd still be here—that boy's like a son to me. But he's got something to give and that's something we need, and *that* makes it fair all around."

"How much is he willing to put into the flotation device?" Bob asked and Mattie could see that the thing was settled.

"Where does that leave you, Mattie girl?" Sam murmured. He had finished flemishing down the braided nylon line and now his hands hung open and empty between his knees.

She said nothing, just leaned forward so that the heavy golden wave of her hair brushed across her shoulders to hide her face.

"Holding the short end of the stick is what it sounds like," he answered himself softly. "Gramps sure has got a great store set by this Jace Wyatt. Me, I don't know. We'll just have to see, won't we?"

The note of quiet finality in his voice brought Mattie's head around.

"Sam! You're not thinking of leaving, Sam?"

He looked at Gramps and Bob busily planning things in the deckhouse. His round, calm, strong face was remote and thoughtful.

"Seventeen years I been with Gramps," he said quietly. "Been good years. But this is a whole new ball game. I never was one to collect things, duffle bag's all I need if I feel like traveling. If this Jace Wyatt's not to my taste, well, I think I'll just be moving on, Mattie."

"Sam, no!" she whispered, appalled.

All her life seemed to be falling to pieces around her, arbitrarily shaken into a new pattern she did not want.

The only stability she had ever known had come when Gramps had taken her in at fourteen at the time of her parents' deaths in a car crash, just as he had taken in teenage runaway Bob Stayner one night, the way one takes in a half-starved alley cat. Bob had stayed to be big brother and mentor to Mattie, and he and Gramps had provided the continuity that Mattie had needed. But it was Sam who had been the bedrock beneath Bob's and Gramps's preoccupation with their own pursuits, Sam who had been nurse and teacher and confidant these past ten years.

"You have to let things go, Mattie," he said gently to her now. "Something else you have to learn."

"I learned that long ago, Sam," she said quietly.

Even if Jace Wyatt turned out to be all that Gramps thought he was, things would never be the same again.

So you let it go—and you dealt with the things that came in its place and you tried to make something for yourself out of them.

Her head came up.

"Gramps. Hey, Gramps!"

"Yeah, Mattie?"

"Is the *Queenfisher* part of the deal?" She meant the sportfisherman she and Sam had salvaged and rebuilt into one of the most trustworthy boats around.

Gramps looked around, shaggy brows raised. "You know the *Queen*'s all yours, Mattie. You earned her."

"Can I have that in writing?"

"Isn't my word good enough?"

"Only if you can speak for Jace Wyatt," she retorted.

He shook his head resignedly. "All right, Mattie. If it's paper you want, paper you'll get."

"And a slip for her."

"Hell, Mattie, that berth on the end of the dock's been hers for six years! You want a lease for that too?" He sighed as she nodded. "Shoo, girl, you can be a pain. Dollar a year for the next ninety-nine years. That suit you?"

"Suits me fine," she said, grinning.

He gave her a puzzled, exasperated glance and turned back to Bob.

"What are you up to, Mattie?" Sam asked.

"Just protecting my interests."

He looked at her quizzically and she laughed under her breath.

"Nothing says I can't go into business for myself, does it?" she said softly. "People come around asking to charter a boat, who do they ask for to be captain and crew? Gramps? Bob? No, it's you and me, Sam. I'm the best skipper around here, even Gramps says so, and you're the best crew."

Sam was chuckling to himself. "You've got a wicked mind, Mattie."

"And I know how to run a business. I've been running this one for years. If Gramps thinks Jace Wyatt can do better, well, here's Wyatt's chance to prove it."

"Gramps is not going to like this," Sam said, grinning.

"I know. I owe him. But I also owe something to myself, Sam."

He nodded. "Yeah, it's about time you set up for yourself."

"Will you come in with me, Sam?"

She held her breath while he thought.

"Don't know about this Jace Wyatt," he said slowly, "but I sure don't mind working for you, Mattie."

Mattie laughed with relief. "It's a risk, Sam. And Gramps is going to be awful mad at both of us for a very long time."

"That don't bother me none." He straightened to his feet, chuckling. "For a little bitty slip of a thing, you got guts, Mattie girl. It'll work."

"Damn right," she said, copying Bob, and Sam laughed and stepped soundlessly onto the pier and went away, still chuckling.

"It's going to be an interesting summer," Gramps said at the door of the deckhouse and Mattie jumped because that was exactly what she had been thinking. Except she was thinking of it as stormy weather ahead.

"It's not going to be as easy as you think," Bob warned. "The flotation idea's still a risk. We've got a long fight ahead."

"That's all right. Jace always liked a good fight."

But Jace Wyatt was sick of fighting.

He had woken once again from a dream of falling—falling and drowning in saltwater and a blaze of white light and pain, fathoms deep.

He leaned on one elbow on the sagging motel bed, trying to control his breathing, then recognized his surroundings and wiped the cold sweat from his face with the back of his arm.

He was used to waking with that shock of violent negation. After a moment, his breathing steadied, he rolled out of bed and went to duck his head under the cold-water tap.

Not long until morning. Morning—and after all these months he could start living again.

Months of waiting in the half-life of base hospital. Enduring the operations, gritting his teeth through the minor hell of the physiotherapy exercises, saying yes ma'am, yes sir, sticking it out because he knew it would all pay off in the end—and it had.

Patience and endurance. The hard lessons painfully learned. There wasn't room in the close quarters of a submarine for temperament. You contained your anger, you rolled with the punches and you waited it out.

Patience and endurance always paid off. It had this time, too, with him back on his feet and fit for anything.

Except the navy.

He clenched his teeth on the sudden surge of bitterness and resentment. You played the hand you were dealt and that was all there was to it. No matter that you had put your life into the navy, no matter that you'd given up too much to it....

Ellie.

Five years since the wreck of his marriage and still the pain slashed out at unexpected moments as sharp and cutting as when it had just happened.

He had understood about Ellie. He had been at sea too long and too often; he couldn't blame her for wanting a husband who was there more than a couple of weeks every three or four months.

Understanding, that came easy for him; forgiveness did not.

He moved restlessly to the window, leaned there, watching the deserted highway, waiting for dawn.

Not that Ellie had slept around behind his back. Long before that happened, she had come and told him straight that she wanted out. She had been honest, as Ellie always was. But he had felt betrayed.

It was irrational to feel anger and betrayal at the fact that she was only human and he had asked too much of her. But knowing that didn't change the way he felt. Other women stuck it out. She had let him down, his bright shining Ellie. The pain was still there, and the anger, and the disinclination to trust in anyone's loyalty.

You couldn't trust anything to last forever. Not navies. Not people. Not even your own body, which could give out on you at any moment.

The sun was coming up behind the dusty palmettos on the other side of the street. He stood looking out the window for a while—Florida was new to him—then went to shower and shave, taking his time because there was no longer any need for speed.

No schedules, no duties—no real purpose. It was alien to him to be at loose ends. All his life he had known exactly where he was going. To have time on his hands, to have no real goal, was insult added to injury, was the thing he found most bitter.

He changed into the civilian clothes that still felt strange to him even after all the months in the hospital, then went around the room, collecting his things and packing them with automatic neatness into his seabag.

Not much to show for all these years. But the rest of it was in his head and his quick clever hands, in the discipline and the skills he'd learned over the past fourteen years.

He took his time driving down the Overseas Highway to Key Vaca. It was past ten by the time he ran his rental car past the Faro Blanco Marine Resort and along to the small pier some distance down the gulf side of the key.

A weather-beaten sign on the dilapidated shack acting as an office read: Sawyer Salvage and Charter. Beyond the shack lay a T-shaped pier. There were a lot of slips along the pier, some filled, but most were empty. A sprawling, solidly built two-story house was off to one side; a little way down the beach was a somewhat newer beach cottage. No one was in sight.

He looked around with an unexpected flicker of interest. All he had expected, all he wanted, was a life he could find barely supportable. No highs or lows, but he could live with that. It was lonely, maybe, but he was used to loneliness. He had been lonely most of his life, even with Ellie because there were always things one couldn't tell Ellie, not unless one wanted to mar the sunshine that was somehow Ellie's due.

But here, under the general air of dilapidation, there were possibilities. The pier was structurally sound under its peeling paint, the machinery and equipment were well cared for, and he could see where the money went: where it should, into those immaculate boats riding at anchor.

The office was empty. So was the house when he banged on its open door.

Then the throb of an engine caught his attention and he looked around to see the forty-foot sportsfisherman coming in to dock.

She was a big shiny white craft with the customary outriggers and flying bridge, and her captain was a slender child in jeans and a man's blue work shirt, faded and thin from many washings. The girl expertly swung the big boat into position, cut the engines at exactly the right moment to bring the boat drifting in to fetch up without a bump against the dock fenders.

He caught a glimpse of the softly rounded oval of her face before the curtain of her honey-gold hair swung to hide it. Winged brows, straight nose, evenly closed lips above a round stubborn chin, a baked-in saltwater tan like poured honey over the sweetly curving flesh.

Then she turned her head and looked down at him—and her eyes, level, wry, faintly smiling eyes with their deep and private amusement, were not a child's. The youthfulness was illusory: it was a woman looking at him, quiet and steady and strong.

He felt a jarring shock of something like recognition, almost stepped back with the surprise of it.

"Make her fast, would you?" she called and tossed him the bowline.

He picked it out of the air, wordlessly drew the boat in, dropped the loop over one of the big dock cleats. Her voice was a warm sound that matched the honey of her tan and the smile in her eyes. She slid down the ladder, disdaining the treads, feet braced expertly against its sides, crossed to throw him the stern line, and stood watching him as he made that one fast. Her quiet gaze looked him over with a level directness that he found unsettling because it made him too aware of her.

"You looking for a boat, mister?"

He straightened, looking up at her. "I'm looking for Alan Sawyer—Gramps." His voice was curt, betraying his irritation.

"He's in town; should be back soon. You can wait or you can talk to me. I captain the boats."

"You?"

His surprise showed. The one word came out too harsh and too abrasive. She didn't look more than twenty, with those slight bones and skin so fine that even at close range in the bright morning light he could see no texture or grain.

"Me," she said, unoffended, with no change in the easy friendliness of her smile, so confident of her competence that she felt no need for defensiveness. No child, this, but a woman, beautiful and strong and at the moment dryly amused. She put one foot up on the gunwale, tucked her thumbs into the belt of her jeans. "I'm the best; take my word for it. But if you've got a problem about that, you can try Harlan's charter. Half mile that way."

"I got no problems, lady," he said, clipped. "And I don't want to hire a boat."

"Then what *do* you want?" she asked reasonably with no awareness of the potential double meaning of the words.

But he found himself thinking of the double meaning, and found himself getting embarrassed because of the thought, and then angry and resentful because of that. The last thing he needed was to get the hots for some little beach bunny not much more than half his age.

"The key to the beachhouse over there," he said shortly.

Her eyes widened. "Wyatt?"

"That's the name, Sawyer."

"Thornton," she corrected absently. "Mattie Thornton. Alan Sawyer's my grandfather on my mother's side."

She had stopped smiling. The level blue eyes had become shuttered and empty, as if the person behind them had quietly retreated behind steel walls. That was the way he wanted it, and yet he found himself irritated.

The irritation must have shown because she made a small, embarrassed movement.

"I'm sorry. Was I staring? You're not what I expected."

"And what was that, Miss Thornton?"

"Oh..." She made a dismissive gesture and smiled faintly. "Welcome to Key Vaca, Mr. Wyatt. We weren't expecting you for another week. The place isn't ready yet, but the guest room in the main house is vacant. You can move your gear right in and we'll have the beach-house fixed up by tomorrow. Is that okay?"

"I don't want to put you to any trouble."

"No trouble," she said, smiling. "Gramps will be on top of the world. Can you wait? He'll be back any minute."

"I'll wait."

"Good." She bent forward, put her hand on his shoulder for balance and jumped lightly down onto the pier.

It was an unthinking, completely impersonal movement, yet he flinched from it. His recoil threw her off balance so that she staggered on landing, stumbled against him. He caught her elbow instinctively to brace her, then feeling her against him, found his fingers tightening to hold her where she was.

For a moment they were still, staring at each other.

She was small, her head barely clearing his shoulder. He was intensely aware of her slender supple body against his, her slight weight, the thrust of her breasts against his rib cage, interestingly mobile under her thin shirt as she tried to push away from him. She smelled of saltwater and engine oil and her own woman scent, a startling combination to be so unexpectedly erotic.

The color was rising in her face now and her eyes had widened, acknowledging the awareness between them, a mutual awareness it seemed from the catch of breath between her parted lips and the insistent pressure of her hand on his chest thrusting for release.

He let her go as if he had been burned and stepped back, snatching at the torn shreds of his usual control. He hadn't acted that way since he was a teenager and even eight months of confinement at the base didn't excuse it.

"Sorry," he said, not looking at her.

"No," said Mattie, confused and blushing. "My fault. I . . . I must have tripped."

She turned away abruptly, trying to get her breath back. It seemed to have been knocked right out of her. She had never felt this way before, and it shocked and bewildered her. She could still feel his body against hers, as if the feel of him were imprinted into her skin—the deep muscles hard and resilient, the bones broad and solid, the size of him overlapping her all around, the hard strength of the grip on her elbow holding her against him.

Jace Wyatt.

He had caught her eye when she had not known who he was, when he had stood looking up at her as she brought the *Queenfisher* in, his face hard with something like irritation. Handsome, that face, with its strong bones, its black slash of brows vivid over the narrow cuts of his eyes, the high cheekbones, the set bitter beautiful mouth.

Standing tall and solid and earthy, feet firmly planted on the pier, he had impressed her. None of the usually wealthy, often powerful men who came to charter their boats had ever done that. It was not his manner, which was quiet, nor his clothes, which were simple—cords, a black crew-necked jersey, a waist-length olive-drab windbreaker. What it was was that feeling of quiet competence, of sure, unshakable, enduring strength.

Gramps is right, she thought; Gramps has lucked in on this deal. This man was not going to walk away when the going got tough, when he found as Mattie had found all the problems and the decisions being dumped on his shoulders. This man was bedrock.

Gramps yelled to him from the end of the pier and Jace turned, and the hard resistive face dissolved into warmth and genuine affection and a pleasure as uncomplicated as a child's. She was so taken aback she could only stand and stare while the two men embraced.

"Let's have a look at you!" Gramps exclaimed. "My God, you've filled out some!"

Jace grinned at him, a white flash of teeth, sudden creases slashing down his cheeks with the smile. "Couldn't say that about you."

"Yeah, I seem to get skinnier the older I get. Hey, have you met Mattie?"

Jace nodded to her, his face hardening, becoming wary. "We've met."

Mattie smiled back stiffly, still wordless from the effect he had had on her, still unable to come to terms with her own reactions. I put my hands on him and I wanted to go on touching him, she thought in bewilderment. She had never felt that way before.

"Come on into the house," Gramps was saying. "We gotta celebrate."

"Let me get my gear from the car."

Mattie watched him walk back to the road. He was about thirty-two, she judged; his body had that solid heavy weight and depth of muscle that comes with maturity. It was an athlete's body, wide-shouldered and lean hipped. He moved with the lazy heavy fluidity of some big cat, only the faint stiffness of his back marring that slow powerful grace. She had seen that deceptive slowness before, knew it capable of very fast and very precise action.

I like the way he moves; I like the way he feels, she thought, and her lips tightened; her face hardened in rejection. Attraction was something new to her, an unknown in her guarded, defensive life, a danger.

"C'mon, c'mon," Gramps urged as Jace came back with his seabag. "Man, I've got a heap of questions. You sure didn't say much in your letters from that hospital. Musta had a fine time there. All them pretty nurses keep you busy, boy?"

"Yeah," said Jace, but his eyes were shuttered and his mouth twitched betrayingly at one corner.

"Shall I break out the champagne, Gramps?" Mattie asked lightly.

"Hell, no!" exclaimed Gramps, distracted. "What do we want with that sody pop? Break out the booze, girl!"

"Sure, Gramps."

She went ahead, aware of Jace's hard stare on her back. She was not sure herself what had prompted her to divert Gramps like that. Only—that stay at the hospital had not been an easy one, anyone could see that, and Jace Wyatt was not ready to talk about it.

As she came abreast of the office, Len Daviot poked his head around the door and waved to her.

"Hey, Mattie, wait up."

She smiled at him. Len was their best customer, spending every other weekend on one of their boats, a cheerful pleasant man they all liked.

"Hi, Len. Want to take a boat out?"

"Yeah, with you and Sam as crew. Only Bob says you've gone into business for yourself."

"That's right. Me, Sam and the *Queenfisher*."

"Well, you, Sam and the *Queenfisher* know where the fish are. You free tomorrow?"

"All day," she nodded, and he grinned with satisfaction.

"Right. Usual time then."

"Dammit!" said Gramps explosively, watching him go, and Mattie laughed out loud. Gramps glared at her. "You're undercutting my business, girl."

"I can handle only one customer at a time, Gramps. That leaves you plenty."

"Yeah, but they're all asking for you!"

"What's going on?" Jace asked behind them.

"Mattie got this fool idea about setting up in business on her own. I didn't think it would make no difference, but half the charters are asking for her. And then there's the paperwork—the orders and the payables and God knows what else. Bob and me got no experience. Mattie's the one who was looking after things. Hell, it's only been a week and a half since she done it and the whole place is coming apart."

"A week and a half?"

Mattie looked away from the tight frown in his eyes.

"She got her nose out of joint when she heard you were coming," Gramps said scornfully. "That was it, wasn't it, Mattie?"

"No, Gramps, it wasn't."

"Don't give me that. It was spite, pure and simple. Spite and a kid's jealousy."

"Have it your own way, Gramps," Mattie said calmly. She looked at Jace and felt the antagonism spark, guarded and wary, between them. "Whatever Gramps thinks, I'm not holding any grudges. You *are* welcome here, Mr. Wyatt."

He inclined his head stiffly in acknowledgment, but his eyes were narrow and disbelieving.

As soon as she could, Mattie made an excuse to leave them. As long as she was present, Gramps remembered his grievance and scowled and frowned. Also she was too aware of Jace, an intrusion in the calm tenor of the house, too big, too vivid, too forceful behind his quiet.

He was aware of her too—she could see that in the tilt of his head, the stiffness of his back and shoulders. She was glad when she had to leave for her afternoon charter. Sexual awareness crackled in the air between them, moved in her blood like a virus, alien and frightening and seductive.

When she came back to make dinner, Bob had arrived and Gramps had recovered his usual ebullience.

She stayed in the background while they talked, listening with interest as the conversation moved from salvage to service stories to Bob's flotation device. Gramps and Bob hardly noticed her moving quietly around them, refilling their plates, refreshing their glasses, listening, watching.

Jace noticed. She was aware of the sideways flicker of his eyes as she passed him, even with her back turned she felt his dark glance, hard and probing. After a while she found herself moving out onto the porch to avoid it.

Bob finally went up to bed around midnight, protesting that he was already dead on his feet. They had done some pretty solid drinking to go along with the service stories and the plans, but Jace showed no effects of it and Gramps had barely scratched the surface. He was up in the attic, energetically rooting through trunks in search of some old photographs.

Jace came and leaned in the open doorway to the porch, his shoulder against the doorjamb, hands in his pockets and his head down, eyes watching her with that up-from-under cat stare that was already becoming familiar.

"We have to talk," he said.

Mattie stopped her restless pacing and looked at him.

"Do we?" she asked provokingly, her eyes mocking and heavy lidded.

She saw the flicker in his, the faint tightening of his face.

"How old are you?" he asked abruptly.

She laughed under her breath. "Yes. It's about time you asked. I'm twenty-four."

His lips pressed sharply together into a grim straight line. "You look..."

"I know how I look," she said dryly. "That's why no one takes me seriously. Gramps calls me his golden child. That's right," she said ruefully to the movement of amusement in his face. "That way he can avoid thinking of me as capable of judgment and avoid having to deal with my opinions. It's easier to think of me as a sandy-rumped little beach bunny throwing a tantrum at being ousted from her place in the sun."

"You're an adult," he said wryly to the irony in her tone.

They looked at each other in silence, eyes guarded.

"I didn't mean to cause trouble," he said abruptly. "When Gramps suggested I buy into the business, I didn't think anyone would object."

In the midst of pulling a wicker chair around, Mattie turned sharply. "I don't, Jace!"

His brows rose disbelievingly.

"It was time for me to break away," she said. "You were just the catalyst."

"You'd better explain that."

Mattie looked at him, at the quiet reassuring strength in his face, the unobtrusive wide-ranging intelligence that saw things that Gramps and Bob never would.

She nodded abruptly, sat down, put her sandaled feet up on the porch railing. He came and leaned on the rail in front of her and she felt the warmth of his hip against her feet, felt a sudden crazy desire to rub her foot against him.

"It goes back to my parents. It's a long story."

His mouth twisted at one corner. "I've got time."

"Okay," she shrugged and smiled crookedly at him. "They married at eighteen and I guess they never grew up. We lived high—but all on plastic, on credit. We never stayed anyplace more than three months and when we moved it was because we had to skip town one step ahead of the bill collectors."

She was silent for a few minutes and he watched her, his eyes intent on her brooding face.

"Funny. I was the only one who worried. I used to be scared stiff of a knock on the door—because it meant strangers shouting and threatening and my mother in tears. Then we'd leave town and it would all be sunshine and laughter again."

"Till the next time."

"Yes."

"You grew up early," he said and she saw that he understood what she was saying.

"Someone had to." She shook her head, dismissing it. "Then one day they piled up their rented Stingray and Gramps came and got me. And then there was this new thing: stability. I didn't know till then that was what I wanted."

"I'm no threat to that, Mattie."

"No. *You're* not. Look, Jace," she said intensely, "I thought I had the life I wanted. I had the sea and the boats and a business I thought was secure. Only—I didn't have it."

He frowned, watching her.

"*I* didn't, Jace. Gramps did. And he could sell it or give it away, and where did that leave me?"

"I'm not going to change things, Mattie."

"No, but you could. I don't want to be dependent on anyone's whims anymore. The only way to be sure your life is going the way you want it to is to take full responsibility for it. So I did."

"You're older than Gramps will ever be," he said wryly and she laughed in surprise.

They understood each other. They were strangers, but underneath in some essential, indefinable way they were alike.

I like him, Mattie thought. She had not expected to and it frightened her a little. But her gaze lingered on him as he leaned there against the railing.

He had discarded his jacket, and the thin blue-black jersey he wore beneath clung to the supple, powerful musculature of his shoulders, his chest and his flat stomach, the crewneck hugging the strong column of his neck, and the sleeves pushed up to bare the muscles of his forearms. It gave her pleasure just to look at him, a slow melting relish, tense and languid at the same time.

He was watching her too, his gaze hooded and brooding.

"Is that all you want out of life?" he asked. "To live in this backwater, run the boats, take care of Gramps?"

"Why not?" She looked at him through half-closed, smiling eyes. "What's better?"

The tone of their voices, lowered, faintly mocking, edged with that hidden sexual antagonism, turned the simplest words charged and intimate.

"Marriage?" he suggested.

"Someday my prince will come?" she mocked.

"I see you don't believe in fairy tales," he said, smiling. "Maybe you're lucky."

"That means you did once," she murmured.

He nodded. "Married seven years. Divorced five."

"What happened?"

He looked away, lips tightening. "She got tired of being alone."

End of subject.

There was an uncompromising loyalty behind his brevity, and a wry weary understanding. No blame cast, no aspersions made, responsibility accepted. Mattie was impressed.

It had hurt him; he was the type of man to be hurt by something like that. He cared.

"I like being alone," she said lightly, twisting the words around so that they became casual, trying to ease the tension in his face. "The beach and the ocean, that's all I need. What do you need, Jace?"

There was a little silence. She saw the movement of bitterness in his eyes as he glanced down at the olive-drab jacket slung over the railing.

"Aside from that," she said gently and his glance came up to her face, black and burning. Then the corner of his mouth twitched betrayingly and he looked away.

"Not much more than I have. A few friends, some space, time to find out who I am, what I want."

"The education of Jace Wyatt," she murmured, smiling, and he laughed with genuine amusement under his breath.

Gramps called her from inside the house and they both looked around.

"I'd better see what he wants," she said and got up.

But he was leaning on the railing directly in front of her and when she rose, she found herself almost brushing him. His palm cupped her elbow, steadying her. Then suddenly they were both still.

He was sitting on the railing and his outstretched legs were a trap on either side of her. His hard face was on her level, so close that she could see the rough texture of his skin, the tiny vulnerable lines fanning from the corners of his narrow eyes out over the distinctive cheekbones. His lids lifted and she was looking straight into the intense darkness of his eyes, falling into the endless blackness.

His hand tightened on her elbow, drawing her to him. His glance dropped to her mouth, the curve of her throat, the swell of her breasts—and she felt his glance like a touch, like a hand pressing into her flesh. Her breath caught.

She felt a shudder of heat, unexpected and totally alien to her, ripple through her body—like the warning breath of a hurricane long before the storm, like the crackle of electricity in the air before the heat lightning.

Her hands had risen to rest upon his chest; his fingers were light on her elbow. Wherever they touched, flesh burned. Her body was heavy and languid, beginning to lean toward him; her breath came short and fast between her parted lips.

"Jace," she whispered in a kind of panic. "Jace, let me go."

The sound of her voice broke the spell. He started abruptly. He too had been caught up in that blood-heavy daze. His glance shot up to her widened eyes. Then faint color brushed his high cheekbones and he let her go with a jerk.

Mattie fled.

Two

—————

Jace was busily installing pumps on the afterdeck of the small trawler Bob had leased when Mattie brought the *Queenfisher* in. He glanced across at her with his wry, crooked smile, no more than the brief rueful lift of the right corner of his mouth, and went back to his work.

They had been quietly avoiding each other for the past two weeks. But distance made no difference to Mattie's awareness of him. Everywhere she looked, he seemed to be there, that quiet contained presence somehow very visible, that energetic weariness strikingly at odds with the easygoing life here on Key Vaca.

"He's got that installation damn near finished," Sam remarked beside her. "Moves fast when he wants to. Fast and sure."

Mattie gave a little irritated grunt and he grinned.

"Have you noticed Bob and Gramps lately? Ask Jace, they say anytime a body wants anything. Sound familiar, Mattie?"

It did. A while ago it was: ask Mattie.

Sam was chuckling under his breath. "Takes a little getting used to, don't it, Mattie?"

"Oh, shut up, Sam," she growled and he laughed.

She was jealous, Mattie admitted honestly to herself. She didn't need Sam's teasing to point out to her that her nose was out of joint. Without in any way wanting it to happen, Mattie had taken a certain childish satisfaction in the fact that the place had fallen to pieces the minute she stopped running things. It had been a boost to her ego to have Bob and Gramps finally stop taking her for granted.

Then Jace had come and without even thinking they had shifted all responsibility to him. It almost added insult to injury that Jace never noticed, that he dealt with everything they threw at him with automatic, unthinking competence and took it as completely natural that he should have to make all the decisions, shoulder all the burdens.

Whatever he and Gramps said to the contrary, he was already making a change in their lives. He seemed incapable of sitting still. The dock had been newly painted, the books had never been in such immaculate order and every piece of machinery on the place ran like a song. Mattie found it exasperating.

He was an intrusion she could not successfully ignore. His dark powerful figure burned constantly on the edge of her vision. Even far out in the blue-green clarity of sea and sky, he was the ghost behind the darkness of her eyelids.

She didn't want to look at him. But she did. And always found his dark eyes looking back, before his eyelids contracted in irritation and his glance flicked away.

"I'll help the Daviots get unloaded," Sam said and padded away aft.

Mattie docked the *Queenfisher*, then looked over at Jace and hesitated, repressing a swift, unwary flash of pleasure at the sight of him.

He was wearing white shorts and a dark blue jersey, and his feet were bare as he padded back and forth between pier and deck. Her glance lingered on the strong clean lines of his body, the flow and flex of the muscles of his back under the thin jersey as he worked, the long powerful legs with their light scattering of hair, the taut buttocks. At rest or in motion, he was beautiful to see.

Those sure, confident movements had a grace of their own unmarred by the stiffness of his back. That unstressed, unthinking efficacy made everything he did look easy, was so natural to him that he was not even conscious of it, took it for granted. He radiated strength and confidence, but would have been startled if she had told him so.

Aware of her gaze, he looked up at her, eyes narrowing under frowning brows. She looked away.

Bob and Gramps were nowhere in sight, both out on charter judging from the empty slips where the two open shoal-draft fishing boats were usually docked. All the small daysailers were also gone, presumably on bareboat charter, so it looked as if it had been a good day all around.

She had to pass Jace on her way to the shack that served as their office. He was down on the pier, manhandling a heavy drum of some unidentifiable liquid onto a sling, and seeing it, she stopped.

"What is that stuff?"

He slanted her a wry grin. "Don't ask me. Some of Bob's special gunk."

Interest aroused, Mattie followed him up the gangway to inspect the heavy machinery weighing down the *Marilee*'s afterquarter.

"That looks awful."

Jace nodded. "Spoils the look of her, doesn't it? But if this test works out, Bob's going to buy her, turn her into a workboat. We'll be able to get the tanks permanently below decks then."

He took up the slack from the hoist, began to haul the heavy drum onto the trawler. With pleasure, Mattie watched the muscles of his back flex under the clinging material of his jersey, then saw the stiffening of his spine as it reacted to the weight.

Instantly she moved to help, her small strong hands catching hold of the line on either side of his.

"Damn it, Mattie!" Jace snapped. "I'm not crippled!"

"Do you think I wouldn't be helping if it were Bob?" she asked mildly and his tight face relaxed.

But she was sorry she had moved to help. She was too aware of their bodies brushing as they hand-over-handed the line, found her gaze lingering on the vulnerable underside of his lifted jaw, the exposed curve of his throat, found herself wanting to put her hands on him. She was glad when they had lifted the drum level with the gunwale and she was able to move away from him to swing it inboard.

He lowered it to the deck, came over to help her unhook the sling.

"Mattie."

He touched her hand lightly. His fingers were long, blunt tipped, cool, his touch precise.

She looked up to see the dark eyes narrowed, the planes of his face a little set.

"Sorry."

Mattie shook her head. "I can't blame you for being fed up with people doing things for you."

His glance dropped. He bent to detach the sling. "You're perceptive."

"It doesn't need much perception to know it was no picnic at that hospital," she said and her voice shook a little.

She was looking at the base of his spine, where the jersey had ridden up when he'd bent over the drum. The small of his back was a network of seamed scars.

He looked up sharply at the note in her voice, then glanced involuntarily over his shoulder. His lips tightened. He straightened abruptly, pulling the jersey roughly down to hide the scars.

"Does it still hurt?" She met his flat stare, her gaze level and steady. "I wasn't trying to pry. Just asking."

Jace looked at her for a moment in stony silence. Then the resistive tension eased out of his face. The corners of his mouth twisted wryly.

"Yeah, it hurts," he said on a long breath almost of relief and sat down on the edge of the drum. It was a kind of surrender.

"You don't have to talk about it," she said and meant it.

"I can't keep ducking every time people ask questions," he said and she saw from the rueful slant of his smile that he was thinking of Gramps.

"Gramps said the trouble is you're still carrying some hardware around with you," she said, keeping her tone

light, and moved to lean companionably against the rail
next to him.

He smiled faintly. "You could say that." He held up
a hand, finger and thumb slightly apart. "There's a piece
of metal about this big in my spine. It stiffens my back
a little, but doesn't interfere with my movements anymore."

"But it did once."

"Yes." Then, as she waited patiently for more, he said
reluctantly, "I was in the hospital eight months. First flat
in bed so that a wheelchair looked like a step up when I
graduated to it after that first operation. Then they did
two more operations and a lot of physiotherapy and I'm
back on my feet."

She was aware of everything he was leaving out—the
fear and the despair and the endless dragging pain. The
terror of helplessness and confinement. The sickening
disappointment after each operation that failed. The
agony she knew physiotherapy for the back was. It was
there in the tightening of his face, the darkness behind
his eyes. But that was something else one didn't men-
tion.

Without even being aware of the movement, she
touched his shoulder lightly. He looked down at her
hand, then sharply up at her face, his eyes narrowing
into unreadable slits.

"What about the piece that's left?" she asked. "Can't
they get it out?"

He took her hand from his shoulder, looked down at
it. She tightened her fingers around his broad palm, re-
fusing to allow him to put his wall back up, and his hand
closed suddenly on hers, enveloping it. The contact became a trusting, confiding link between them.

"Jace," she insisted, "can't they do anything?"

He looked up at her, his eyes wry and smiling.

"Short of a spinal transplant?" It was a joke and she smiled back, giving him the space he needed. His hand tightened on hers, shook it slightly, reassuringly, then let it go. "No."

"Why not?"

"It's imbedded in the bone," he said simply.

"Gramps said the wrong kind of strain could make it shift."

"That's right."

"What would happen then?"

He looked up at her, his gaze flat and hard. "If I survived it?"

She caught her breath. The deliberation in his voice made his purpose unmistakably clear. Nothing permanent, he was saying, and this was the reason why.

He saw that she understood, and ducked his head, his face relaxing now that the warning had been given. She appreciated his honesty—even though she thought he was wrong.

"Back in the wheelchair doing physiotherapy exercises, I guess," he said, throwing it away.

But she knew as surely as if he had spoken that he would prefer the other. He was the kind of man who would find confinement insupportable.

"That's a hard thing to live with," she said quietly.

"No choice."

She saw that he had come to terms with it long ago, and recognized the strength that enabled him to accept and deal with it.

"You've got more guts than I have," she said. "That's like carrying around a live bomb that could go off any second. I'd be scared stiff."

"Men aren't supposed to be scared," he said with a flicker of amusement.

Mattie laughed out loud. "Come off it, Wyatt."

They grinned at each other.

"I'm scared," he agreed, smiling. "But you can't let that stop you."

"Go on with your life," she murmured.

"That's right." His glance came up, level and hard. "Only you don't make long-term plans and you don't trust anything to last forever."

She was silent a moment, watching him. "That's a pretty sweeping statement, Jace."

"Maybe. But that's the only way I know how to operate."

They looked at each other in silence. It had needed to be said.

"Mattie?" Len Daviot's voice interrupted. "Are you free for another charter this Friday?"

She looked around, startled. She hadn't even heard him come up.

"Yes, I am, Len," she said, recovering herself.

"Sounds like you had a good day," Jace remarked and Len grinned.

"Sure did. You Gramps's new partner?"

"That's right. Jace Wyatt."

"Len Daviot." They leaned forward to shake hands across the gunwale. "It was a great day. We raised two sails and connected with a blue marlin in the three-hundred-pound class. Missed both sails and the big boy managed to wrap the leader around his bill, snap it and get away."

Len grinned at Mattie's rueful face.

"My fault, not Mattie's. She's a real gung-ho skipper. If I'd had a little more experience, I'd have taken him."

"Gung ho?" Jace grinned at Mattie. "You don't look it, Mattie."

"I don't look strong either, but I am," she retorted. "Haven't you learned yet that appearances are deceiving, Jace Wyatt?"

He glanced down at her, smiling. "Me, I like the view."

"Prettiest scenery in twenty miles," Len agreed and Mattie blushed. "Cute, isn't she? Makes you want to drop a handkerchief over her when nobody's looking and take her home for a pet."

Mattie's eyes flashed. "You're asking for it, Len."

"Only problem is she swings a mean belaying pin," he said unrepentantly to Jace. "For a small package, she packs quite a punch." He threw up his hands as Mattie reached for the boat hook. "I'm going, I'm going."

"I wondered if you ever had any trouble with your charters," Jace said, amused, as Len bounded away down the pier.

Mattie put down the boat hook, smiling. "Not after I knocked a couple overboard and let them swim around awhile to cool off. Then there's always Sam."

Jace looked over to where Sam's bulk loomed over the Daviots as he put their gear into their car.

"I can see how that might be a deterrent."

"I've got three watchdogs," she said dryly. "Plus every charter-boat skipper from Key Largo to Key West. No one messes with me unless I want it."

He had gone down on one knee to check the pumps. He looked up at her, amused, as he turned on the diesel.

"That's quite a gauntlet your admirers have to run. That why you're still footloose and fancy-free?"

"Now you're prying," she said lightly.

"No," he said quietly. Their glances held for a moment, then he looked back at the oil leak one of the pumps had sprung.

Mattie watched his averted face for a moment. She knew by the sudden tension that he had not intended to ask that question.

Why should she be the only one struggling on that hook of unwilling desire and indecision?

"No one measured up," she said simply.

His glance flashed to her face for an intense second before dropping to the pump.

"Put your thumb over this," he said, his voice a little rough.

She sat down beside him on the deck, her thumb going unerringly to the spurting hole in the oil line, her strong hands holding the pipe steady while he wound tape around it.

The wind blew her hair across his throat as they bent over the pipe, their heads close together. Their shoulders brushed. She could feel the warmth of his body beside hers, the size and strength of him. His hands were twice the width of hers and she found herself looking at them with pleasure. She turned her head to see his jaw set, his face hard with tension, his lips a tight, grim line, their corners faintly pointed with strain.

He was angry with himself and with her, and she understood because that was exactly the way she felt.

He had given her every reason to avoid involvement with him. She should run—fast and far.

But his lashes were spiky on the flat plane of his cheek. The shallow curves of bone just below his eyes were infinitely vulnerable. The darkness in his eyes as they suddenly lifted to hers was an imperative far more potent than common sense.

"Need any help over there?"

Mattie started, realizing that they had been staring at each other for minutes on end, caught up in a kind of urgent, powerful blood heaviness that obliterated all awareness of the world around them.

She looked up, controlling the color rising in her face only by a fierce effort of will.

It was Sam. He was not looking at her. He was looking at Jace and there was a level warning in his eyes.

Jace straightened to his feet, wiping the grease from his hands with a rag. He was smiling faintly and his gaze was steady on Sam's.

"We're through till Bob gets here," he said and Sam nodded.

"Right. Mattie, the boat yards called. They've got those supplies Bob ordered. I'm going over to get them now."

"All right," she said quietly and got to her feet.

Sam gave Jace one more level stare, then turned away. Jace laughed under his breath.

"The watchdogs are effective, Mattie."

Her lids were down, weighty and slumberous over her darkened eyes. Her body felt heavy and languorous, still vibrating to that pulse of blood between them, that beat that came from her heart or his. She was aware of her body as she had never been before, so sensitized was it— of her nipples hard under the rub of her shirt, of her hair whispering across the skin of her throat, of the silken movement of her thighs against the rough denim of her jeans.

"They can be called off," she murmured, gravely mocking.

His body made a sudden movement toward her, his hand gripped her upper arm. Mattie's breath stopped in her throat.

"Don't play games, Mattie," he said between his teeth, and she saw that his face was set and controlled. "I can understand your trying your wings. But don't try them on me. I'm not made of glass. Push me and I'll take you up on it. I've been celibate for eight months and anybody looks good to me now. If a one-night stand's what you're after, I'll be glad to oblige."

He saw the shock in her face and let her go with a careful push.

"You're not that kind, Mattie. But that's all I have to give—and that's not good enough. For either of us. So practice your growing up on someone else."

She met his hard gaze levelly.

"I'm grown, Jace Wyatt," she said gravely. "I think you know that."

She watched his lips part on a harsh, indrawn breath, then turned and walked away from him.

Three

He wanted her. She knew that and the knowledge was at once exhilarating and terrifying. She had never felt this way before—this crazy mix of fear and fascination and reckless, breathless, almost drunken delight.

No one she had met before had ever tempted her past the point of a few dates, a few desultory kisses. She had never experienced this urgent, imperative, elemental blood heat that pounded dizzyingly through her with every beat of her heart, every breath she took.

He made her feel things she did not want to feel. He threatened her careful, hard-won stability. His very existence was a danger, but she didn't care because it was also an irresistible temptation.

She found herself caught by his every word or expression or gesture, found herself entranced, unable to look away. And she knew he watched her, too. She could feel his gaze on her, heavy and reluctant, a dark smolder of rigidly controlled heat, and would find her breath grow short at the brooding sensuality behind it.

Distance would have helped. But distance was not possible. He was always somewhere around, working on the pier, crewing for Bob or Gramps, learning the ropes, becoming part and parcel of their lives.

Gramps wanted him to be part of the family. They all did. It became an accepted thing that he eat his meals with them, spent his evenings lounging around their living room, his hands always tinkering with some piece of equipment and his eyes coming up with that wry amusement at some crack of Bob's or Sam's.

"We must've pumped that fish for hours." That was Gramps, feet on the coffee table, comfortably sprawled, enjoying the unwinding time after dinner when everybody relaxed and chewed the fat and got ready for the next day. "That charter of mine thought he'd died and gone to heaven. How big you'd say that fish was, Jace?"

"I'm no expert."

"Shoo, musta been seven, eight hunnert pounds, easy."

"You manage to land this phenomenon, Gramps?" Bob asked.

"Would he be adding a hundred pounds every time he tells that story if he did?" Jace murmured, his gaze on the air valve he was repairing.

Gramps glared at him while the others laughed.

"Just for that, you ain't coming on my boat tomorrow."

"That'll break him up all to pieces." Sam slapped Jace's knee and they grinned at each other. "You can come with me on the shoal draft tomorrow. You haven't gone poling across the flats yet, bonefishing."

"What's bonefishing?"

They all chipped in to tell him and he listened to them, half smiling, his glance moving reflectively from face to face.

It hurt Mattie's heart to watch him. He was guarded, wary, keeping himself a little removed, always one step outside their circle of warmth and laughter, but unwillingly seduced by it, yielding to them with an untrusting wistfulness that hurt her with its suggestion of both doubt and yearning. He didn't want involvement and yet was tempted by it. She could see the struggle in him and it was the same struggle that was in his eyes when he looked at her.

The phone rang and Bob went into the hall to answer it.

"Hey, Jace," he called after a few minutes. "Tomorrow's Saturday night. Fran says how about we go out on the town, you and Mattie and me and Fran? C'mon, we can have ourselves a real good time!"

Jace's glance lifted sharply to Mattie's face.

"Saturday night's Bob's night to howl," Gramps explained. "We've been too busy these past few weeks, that's why he's so all-fired het up. Sam usually goes along to keep them out of trouble."

"Not this time," Sam said contentedly. "This time Jace can take over the job."

As Sam had appointed himself this family's unofficial guardian, this was an immense vote of confidence. Both Mattie and Jace looked sharply at him. He looked back blandly.

"It won't be bothersome. You just bring Bob home in one piece and keep an eye on the kid here." Gramps jerked a thumb at Mattie. "You won't have to be ashamed of her. She can look right purty in a dress."

"Gramps!" exclaimed Mattie in outrage.

Jace laughed aloud. "That doesn't surprise me. I'd be honored, Mattie."

Seething, Mattie jerked her chin in curt acknowledgment.

Gramps was unobservant. He saw Mattie always and inevitably as ten years old. He wanted Mattie to be kid sister to the son he saw Jace as and never realized that so innocent a relationship was utterly beyond them.

She wanted to knock all their silly, interfering heads together. And she was furious with Jace, Jace and his control and his distance and his insistence in protecting her when she didn't *want* to be protected.

She felt reckless and edgy. She got up and went around the room, collecting glasses. Bob was still on the phone to Fran. Gramps and Sam were in the kitchen, arguing affably over Gramps's insistence on one more beer. Very deliberately she stopped behind Jace, put a hand on his shoulder.

She felt the deep muscles tense under her touch. Then he tipped his head back and looked up at her, his face still and expressionless.

"Don't come if it's going to be such a chore," she said tightly.

"Damn it, Mattie," he said, "you know why...."

"No, I don't know why," she mocked. "Tell me why, Jace."

She bent to take his empty glass from his hand, leaning over him so that her hair fell in a curtain over her face and his. They looked at each other in intense stillness in the lamplit golden cave formed by her falling hair. And deep within the slitted resistive eyes looking up at her was that involuntary flicker of heat, that awareness sparking between them as volatile and dangerous as oil on dry grass.

"Scared, Jace?" she murmured and his hand came up suddenly to grip her hair, drawing her head down, his intent gaze dropping to her mouth.

Then even as she caught her breath, his grip loosened. His fingers slid caressingly through her hair, fell away.

"Yes, Mattie," he said. "I'm scared."

His honesty shamed her.

"I'm sorry."

"You're still playing games, Mattie. You're not sure."

"No, I'm not sure," she admitted ruefully. "But it is tempting to find out."

His hand closed around her wrist, enveloping it, his touch a caress. She turned her arm in his clasp till she could curve her fingers around the broad bones of his wrist. Linked, they looked at each other with an understanding deeper than words.

I don't know anything about him, she thought, and yet I know him, bone-deep, where it counts.

"You're not going to make it easy for me, are you?" he said and his gaze was faintly smiling, black with a tightly contained sensuality.

"To do the right thing?" she mocked. "No."

He laughed under his breath and his glance dropped to their linked wrists. He drew her hand to his mouth—with a shiver she felt his lips move against her flesh—then he was on his feet and moving away from her, his face averted, his profile brooding and withdrawn.

She almost expected him to find some excuse to not come with them the next evening. But when she came down the stairs he was waiting at the foot.

His glance swept her appreciatively from the top of her shining golden head over the gay strapless sundress she wore down to the delicate sandals on her small feet.

"You do look 'purty in a dress,'" he said and grinned as the color rushed up in her face.

"Thank you," she said with restraint. "Is that the best you can do?"

He laughed under his breath. "What do you want, Mattie? Something to the effect that I could drown in the blue pools of your eyes? All those fancy words?"

"Only if you mean them," she said, clipped, and came down the last few steps, expecting him to move away to allow her passage.

But he did not. He stood like a wall blocking her path, and she stopped abruptly just before she walked into him.

His face was level with hers as she stood one step higher than he; his gaze was intent on hers.

And suddenly, because of something in his intense eyes, he was too close. She was too aware of him, the size of him, the strength, straight shoulders splaying past hers, square hips wider than her own, the powerful body overlapping her all around—the solid, sensual reality of him.

That look in his eyes held her still, unable to move as his hand rose. His fingertips brushed her hair, slid across her shoulder, down her bare arm. A light, perfectly innocuous touch, yet her breath caught.

"Oh, I'd mean them, Mattie, all those fancy words." His voice was a rasp in his throat, a nighttime sound, and she shivered involuntarily. His glance moved over her, heavy and lingering, and wherever it rested her flesh burned. "They'd be true. That your skin feels like silk. That a man could lose himself in the net of your hair. That the curve of your throat was meant for a man's mouth...."

Her breath left her in a little rush.

Holding her wide-eyed gaze, he bent his head to the hollow of her shoulder. She felt his open mouth a fraction of an inch from her skin, heard the whisper of his breath drawing in the scent of her. Then he raised his head again, smiling, without having touched her skin.

The small movement was somehow so erotic that her knees turned to water and she had to lean on the banister to avoid going straight down in a heap at his feet.

"Jace, what . . . ?"

His eyes were all laughter and a strange mocking tenderness.

"Two can play at that game, Mattie."

He knew the words, he knew the moves, he had just shown her exactly how inexperienced she really was.

"Stop teasing the animals," he said quietly. And Mattie, confused, breathless, more than a little shaken, knew he was right. She wasn't ready; she wasn't ready at all for the consequences of pushing him past that control of his.

A car horn sounded impatiently outside the house— Bob, getting tired of waiting and impatient to pick up Fran.

Gramps put his head around the kitchen door. "Hey, Jace, did you get that engine fixed? Don't care if you do it tomorrow as long as I have it for Monday."

"It's fixed," said Jace over his shoulder.

"Good to be able to rely on someone around here," said Gramps and Mattie shot him a look of pure irritation.

"Isn't anything difficult for you?" she muttered under her breath and Jace looked down at her, startled.

"Not engines," he said, then frowned. "What are you talking about, Mattie?"

She had meant a lot more than just his gift with anything mechanical. She had meant that quiet, downplayed, wide-ranging intelligence that plotted courses or computed diving formulas with absentminded precision, that swept with almost insulting ease through the account books and financial statements that had always left her sweating gently whenever she had had to deal with them, that was always somehow one step ahead of one whatever subject arose. She found herself resenting him for that, then was ashamed of her own resentment, so was silent.

Over Cuban food at Castillito, she was quiet while the others talked, lost in her own thoughts, trying to understand her own ambivalence.

It wasn't just because desire was new to her. It was because he was a stranger. She knew him and she did not know him. That was the problem. He was always an enigma, his thoughts hidden, his reactions a complete surprise. She could not come to terms with herself until she understood him, but he had retreated behind that wall of silence that none of them could breach.

"How about going to Delkote's?" Bob suggested and she nodded absently, not really listening.

The town was crowded with tourists and locals, all cutting loose in this hot, sprawling, wide-open night. Jace's arm came around Mattie's shoulders, warding off jostling passersby. With anyone else, Mattie would have bristled. She prized her independence and she knew that they would have done it because they thought she could not take care of herself. But looking up at that quiet, brooding face above her, she saw that the movement was unthinking, that with him the protective instinct was as automatic as breathing.

"Where are we going?" he asked, frowning at the increasing seediness of the streets through which Bob and Fran were leading them.

"Delkote's," she answered. "It's got a big dance floor and it stays open till four in the morning. It's all right," she said as he almost balked at the garish purple neon flashing over the purple-and-black door. "It's a dive, but they know us here."

"It's asking for trouble," he muttered and she had to bite her tongue to keep from agreeing. That was usually the reason Bob came here.

They pushed through the doors into a blast of deafening rock music and rapid-fire light flashes. The place was so crowded there was hardly room to breathe. Bob and Fran had already vanished from sight, lost somewhere in the maze of gyrating bodies on the dance floor.

Mattie waved to catch the bartender's eye and he waved back.

"Good God almighty," said Jace. That was everyone's first reaction to Delkote. He was a lanky brown man, impossibly tall with a head shaved cueball clean and a face that could curdle milk.

"Hey," said Mattie, grinning. "He's the owner and very stable. And a friend of Sam's."

At that he relaxed imperceptibly. She laughed, looking up at him as he worked them through the crush, his body folded sideways around her, his shoulder and bent arm clearing the way.

"That reassures you, does it? Think we're helpless without Sam?"

"Honey," he muttered, "the three of you make a man quail. You need a keeper. Sam's the keeper."

That was deliberate provocation. But she saw the amusement in the sideways flick of his eyes toward her and simply laughed at him.

"I'm the keeper, Wyatt. Haven't you realized that yet?"

"Sam does what you say. Yes, I've realized that."

They were both smiling.

It was only a few decibels quieter at the back of the room where Delkote was clearing a table for them, but even that made a difference.

"White wine as usual, Mattie?" Delkote was already setting out drinks.

"Thanks, Del. Where are Bob and Fran?"

"Look north-northwest. See the arm waving the bottle? Yeah. He's made inroads in the first ten seconds." He looked Jace over. "You Wyatt? Sam told me about you. Bourbon, right? Try to keep Bob from tearing up the place, okay? I only just got the mirror fixed."

Mattie laughed at the look on Jace's face as Delkote slid off without waiting for an answer.

"You get used to him."

"In a couple of years. What was that about Bob?" He held her chair for her.

"Oh, every now and then Bob likes to take on all comers."

"Give me strength."

Something in the pocket of his light windbreaker bumped her as he sat down.

"What's that?"

He lifted his arm indulgently to allow her to dip into his pocket. She came up with a paperback, dog-eared and soft with much handling, and tipped it to the light.

"Conrad's *The Shadow Line*?" she remarked in surprise.

He grinned crookedly. "One gets tired of girlie magazines."

"Funny man," she said dryly and he laughed. She was already familiar with his taste in books and Conrad was representative. She could tell from the paperback's condition it had been read and reread, Conrad an old friend, and that pleased her because it was one more thing that they shared. "I love Conrad, that's all. I learned a lot from him, about the sea and about people."

Jace was leaning forward on the table, watching her with half-mocking eyes.

"Is that how you learned about people—through reading?"

Mattie smiled faintly. "That and the microcosm of Key Vaca." She looked at him challengingly. "And you learned about them through reading and the macrocosm of the world. We still arrive at the same point for all I've spent my life in this 'backwater.' "

"Maybe. You've still got a few years to go, twenty-four." Used as a nickname, her age became a gibe. "You're still wearing those rose-colored glasses."

"Is that your definition of maturity, Jace? Cynicism?"

There was a small silence, then: "No," he said. "No. That's just the place where I'm at."

He raised his glass abruptly to his lips, putting an end to the conversation. Mattie looked down at the book in her hands. That last remark had been revealing.

A piece of paper fell out as she riffled the pages, a scrap torn from a mimeographed sheet and folded lengthwise to act as a bookmark. She unfolded it idly. It was part of a test paper of some kind, the last question on that page.

Then her mind took in the sense of the words and she blinked.

"Sketch and describe the control-rod configuration of the main reactor," it read. "Show the relationship between control rod geometry and fuel element geometry. Explain the effect on nuclear flux. Describe the theoretical considerations pertaining to the flux density at various control-post positions...."

"Jace?" she said carefully. "What is this?"

He glanced down, brows lifting, then smiled.

"I didn't realize I'd had that edition that long. I took that test about nine years ago."

"Why would you take a physics test?"

"Not physics. Engineering. Nuclear reactors."

"Nuclear..." said Mattie in a failing voice.

"That's what drives a sub, Mattie."

"Next you'll tell me you could build one from scratch," she muttered, joking to cover the fact that she was impressed, and he grinned.

"Well, not with my bare hands. But I could show a crew how." He was not joking.

Mattie stared at him. "Do all officers have to know this?"

"Command doesn't, but command wasn't my line. Oh, every officer has to take the conn sometime and I have. But my job was to keep the boat running."

"Chief of the boat," she remembered Gramps saying, but she had not known what that meant, the kind of knowledge it entailed.

"I thought you were in underwater demolition."

"Master-at-arms," he nodded. "That was weapons. Demolition was part of that and I had scuba experience. Everyone ends up doing double duty on subs. Something wrong, Mattie?"

She had suddenly realized just how much knowledge was packed into that head of his. All the clues she had overlooked suddenly came together—the quick intelligence, his taste in books, why everything he did around the place had seemed the products of a motor idling. He *was* idling. Nothing around here had required him to even raise his foot to the gas.

"Jace, just what *are* you doing in a little no-account salvage-and-charter business?"

His gaze came up to hers, level and hard, suddenly bleak. "It's useless knowledge, Mattie."

She shook her head dazedly. "But surely..."

"How do I use it, Mattie? Where?"

She did not know. "Why didn't you take a desk job at the base, training people or something?"

"I couldn't have taken the frustration," he said simply. "I had to make a clean break. Try to make a life for myself out of something else."

But this life here on Key Vaca would use not a tenth of his potential and not one particle of his knowledge. And she could see from the bleak stillness in his eyes that he was beginning to realize this himself.

For the first time she understood how cut off and adrift he really was, and her heart went out to him.

"No wonder you find everything here so easy," she murmured, ashamed of her previous resentment.

"There's still the salvage," he said and she heard the barely perceptible note of desperation in the quiet voice.

But the salvage she knew was no more challenging than the charters.

Someone bumped into their table and they looked up in surprise. It was Bob, grinning and swaying a little on his feet.

"Hey, how you two getting on?"

"Great," said Mattie wearily. "Where's Fran?"

"Powdering her nose. Why don't you powder yours, Mattie? It would be a real good idea right about now."

She looked up sharply. His eyes were glittering. The whiskey bottle he set down on the table was empty. But he wasn't drunk. Not yet. Just getting into gear and at that quarrelsome stage all of them knew.

"Jace," she said urgently. Then it was too late to warn him because two men had materialized behind Bob, one a redhead, one a blonde, but otherwise a matched set—brawny, half-drunk and belligerent, just the type Bob liked to roust.

"We've been looking for you," the redhead said.

"Hey," said Bob, grinning, "good to see you. Thought you'd run right outta here."

"What's going on?" Jace asked sharply.

"The guy's got no sense of humor," Bob explained. "I told him he had a face like an ape and he didn't find it funny. Don't you think he has a face like an ape, Jace?"

"What the hell do you think you're doing?" Jace snapped. He had leaned forward so that his shoulder slanted across Mattie, shielding her.

"Come on, punk," the redhead said, interested only in Bob. "Outside."

"He wants to play," said Bob.

Jace came to his feet, moving slow and easy to avoid precipitating events.

"Take it easy, fellas," he said, his voice soft and light and oddly remote. "We don't want any trouble. My friend's drunk."

"Yeah, well, your friend's got a lesson coming to him," the redhead said without moving his gaze from Bob. "Outside."

"He-ey," said Bob, grinning from ear to ear. "What outside? I can take you two mama's boys right here."

"Okay, that's it," said the redhead and grabbed for him.

Jace's stiff arm jolted him back on his heels.

"Back off," he said. His voice had changed, was hard with menace, aimed impartially at the three of them. His face was set and remote.

"It's your funeral," said the redhead.

He swung, fast and hard, and metal glittered in the light, a band across all four fingers.

Mattie shot to her feet, crying out a warning.

But Jace was already ducking. The fist grazed his left cheekbone, brass knuckles cutting a gash across it. Then he was straightening, body swaying smoothly away from the man, then coming back with shocking speed, left elbow rising. That elbow, propelled by the force of his right hand on his left fist, hit the redhead solidly behind his left ear. The blow traveled no more than six inches, but the man fell like a stone.

The speed and efficiency of it immobilized everyone.

Then the blond man gave a hoarse cry and rushed. Jace had already swiveled, the movement a continuation of the blow. His left hand caught the man's wrist, swung it down and around. Spun around, the blond grunted in surprised pain as his wrist slammed between his shoulder blades. Then Jace, continuing that smooth unbroken flow of movement, had his forearm across the man's throat.

Mattie gasped. Bob was paralyzed. They were both in shock from the speed, precision and efficiency of his attack.

Jace stopped.

Everything stopped. The music was still blaring, the lights flashing. But for Mattie, there was just this frozen moment: the two strained figures, the horrified faces of the people at the surrounding tables as they started to their feet, the rasping sound of the blond man struggling for breath, and the deadly, intent, absorbed remoteness of Jace's face.

Then Delkote was there with Eddie, his bouncer. And Fran was behind them both, Fran who had the sense to go for Delkote instead of retreating into the powder room.

"You can let him go now, Jace," Delkote said calmly.

There was a moment of tense silence. Then Jace nodded, his face easing out of that cold, fighter's mask. Moving slowly and carefully, he withdrew his arm from the blond man's throat, then shoved him abruptly at Eddie.

Eddie was as tall as Delkote and weighed two-hundred-and-fifty-plus pounds. He enveloped the man in arms thicker than Mattie's waist and very gently, very firmly, walked him out of the door, ignoring his struggles.

"Thanks," said Delkote to Jace. "You okay?"

"I'm okay," said Jace. He was breathing in deep slow breaths.

Delkote looked at Bob. "Go home, hero," he said softly. "Before I coldcock you."

"Come on, tiger," said Fran, taking Bob's arm. She smiled ruefully at Jace. "He'll be all right now, Jace. Thank you. I'll send him home in the morning."

Jace looked at Mattie. She was standing balanced on the balls of her feet, braced for action, the whiskey bottle she had caught up still held by its neck in her clenched fist.

He looked at the bottle and there was a flicker of appreciation and amusement in his face.

"Would you have used that?"

"Yes," said Mattie firmly. Then: "You're bleeding."

He swiped the back of his wrist across his cheekbone, looked at it with surprise. Like all facial cuts, the slash was bleeding heavily.

"Damn." He accepted the handkerchief Mattie held out, pressed it to the cut. "Does he do that all the time?" he asked, meaning Bob.

"Every now and then," she said resignedly. "I told you."

"Yeah." The one word was taut with irritation.

"Don't be angry."

"You could have been hurt. He should have thought of that. He should have thought of his girl. There's no excuse for starting a fight when the two of you were around to get hurt."

His voice was staccato with residual tension.

"Let's go home," Maggie suggested, hoping to distract him.

But he brooded all the way home, his eyes narrow in his grim face and his mouth a hard line. Bob was going to have a strip torn off him tomorrow. But Bob deserved that and maybe this time it would sink in.

"Come inside," she said when Jace would have turned away after seeing her to her door. "I want to look at that cut."

"It's just a scratch."

"It always is," she said dryly.

He shrugged and followed her into the house. The hall light was on, but the rest of the house was dark. Sam and Gramps must have gone to bed.

Mattie led the way into the kitchen and went straight for the cabinet that held the first-aid box. Jace hitched a hip onto the kitchen table, then sat there looking down at his hands.

She set the first-aid box beside him, soaked a cotton ball in antiseptic.

"Don't be too hard on Bob," she said awkwardly. "I know you've got a right to be angry, but..."

"You know what really burns me up?" he asked, not listening. "It's the pointlessness of it. The stupid, useless waste of it. Getting into a fight just because he's bored and antsy. For God's sake!"

"If you fight, you fight for real," she murmured, finishing his thought.

He jerked his face irritably away as she tried to swab the cut.

"Yes." He caught her wrist as she tried again. "I frightened you, didn't I?"

"Yes," she said honestly.

She studied him gravely and he looked back, his gaze hard and level, unwavering. For the first time she was aware of the violence behind his quiet.

"Are you afraid of me now?" he asked flatly.

"No," she said and meant it. The violence was controlled and that control would not break, not when he saw violence, even the easy thoughtless violence of a bar fight, as something to be avoided, something too important to be taken lightly. This was his center: the conscience and the essential gentleness that reined back that very real strength, that dangerous knowledge.

"Maybe you should be," he said wryly. She saw that
he was angry with himself. "I am. The training took over
and it was all automatic. This movement follows that—
one, two, three. Damn it, Mattie, I could have really hurt
that man."

"But you didn't," she said quietly. "You never will."

He looked up at her, his eyes faintly startled. "You
have a lot of faith in me."

"Yes," she said. "I do."

His hand tightened fractionally about her wrist. His
gaze was intent and searching on her face. She flushed a
little, moved her hand lightly in his grasp.

"Let me see to that cut, Jace."

"It's all right," he said impatiently and winced away
from the tiny sting of the antiseptic, face screwed up like
that of a five-year-old.

It was unexpectedly endearing. She laughed softly
under her breath.

"What's so funny?" he demanded.

"Nothing." She pressed a Band-Aid carefully into
place. "All of a sudden I like you very much, Jace
Wyatt."

His eyes widened in surprise, unsure and suddenly
very young.

She had to suppress a startlingly fierce urge to put her
arms around him. She was starting to understand him
after all, starting to love this complex, exasperatingly
complicated man.

Four

The next morning a very chastened Bob apologized. Mattie was a little taken aback. Whatever Jace had said, it had made an impression because for the first time Bob really meant it.

"Hey, no sweat," she said lightly and he relaxed.

"I'm going to test that flotation device," he said. "I want your help, Mattie."

"Sure."

"And Sam's. Where is he?"

"In town. How about Jace?"

Bob winced and Mattie laughed.

But Jace held no grudges. Once a reaming out was over, it was over.

"Sure," he said easily. "What are you going to do?"

Bob was already off in his head somewhere, thinking only of his process.

"I've sunk our smallest daysailer off the rocks behind your beachhouse," he said. "As a test it's something on the order of a toy boat in a bathtub, but if we can bring her up it's the final proof I need that the process works."

Jace nodded. "What do we do?"

"I've already gone down, got the hoses connected to her. I need you to work the pumps forcing my mix of chemicals down into her while I regulate the flow. Umm." He hesitated, for once aware of something beyond his usual singlemindedness. "It might be kinda hard work, Mattie."

Mattie blinked. "So when did that ever stop me?"

"I should have known," he said and grinned.

"What must you have said," she muttered to Jace as they followed Bob down to the rocks.

"He just doesn't think," Jace said. "Just has to have a few things pointed out to him now and then."

"Well, cut it out," she said irritably. "I don't like being wrapped in cotton wool."

He raised his brows and didn't say a word, and she knew she hadn't gotten through to him at all.

Manning Bob's pumps really was hard work.

"What does this stuff do?" Mattie asked, pumping away till her arm ached. "In layman's terms," she added hurriedly as Bob's eyes lit up with that glow that usually resulted in half an hour's worth of abstruse chemical formulas.

"Oh." He paused, stymied. "Well, that chemical heats the water and those two interact with it. Between the heat and the interaction, all these gases and air bubbles start up in the stuff. When we pump it into the *Mako*'s hull, the cooler water down there will harden it and it'll separate into hundreds of blobs full of air and gas. Then when the *Mako*'s packed full of them, they'll pop her right up to the surface.''

''Oh,'' said Mattie and grinned ruefully as Jace laughed. It sounded far too simple. But then she had asked for that. ''Do *you* believe it'll work?'' she asked Jace.

He was smiling. ''I believe in results,'' he said, avoiding the issue.

''Coward.''

''If I gave you the formulas, you'd see that it has to work,'' Bob protested.

Mattie pointed at a few creamy grapefruit-sized balls bobbing against the rocks on which they knelt.

''Are those what you're talking about?''

''What? Where?'' He peered into the sea. ''Dammit, one of *Mako*'s ventilators must have blown. She'll never come up if they're leaking out of her like that. I'd better go fix it.''

Mattie suddenly saw a rising shape deep within the pellucid water.

''Bob, wait! Bob!''

But he had already dived in.

Mattie went straight after him.

A second later Jace plummeted into the sea beside her.

For one wild moment of confusion there was nothing but a tangle of arms and legs and elbows—Jace trying to shove her out of danger, Mattie struggling to get past him and at Bob who was still intent on the *Mako*.

Then the confusion resolved itself. Mattie twisted forcibly around Jace's warding hand and grabbed Bob's belt just as Jace did. Together they yanked Bob out of the way just as the *Mako* shot past, heading for the surface with all the force of an express train.

Then they were at the surface themselves, gasping for breath, and Jace was shoving them against the rocks and out of the way of the wildly swinging boat.

"It works!" yelled Bob, coughing and beating on the rocks with his fist. "Mattie, Jace! It works!"

"You moron!" shrieked Mattie, blind with residual terror. "You could have broken every bone in your body! She'd have hit you like a freight train coming up like that!"

Bob grabbed her head and placed a smacking kiss on the top of it. Then he broke away from them and kissed the *Mako*. To him the danger he had been in was irrelevant to the fact that the *Mako had* come up.

"It won't do any good to strangle him," Jace said, amused, in her ear. "He wouldn't even know why you're doing it. Are you all right, Mattie?"

"I'm fine." She was coughing, one hand on the rocks for balance, still so angry at Bob that she had no breath. Jace's shoulder came under her armpit, steadying her, lifting her a little out of the water. His arm was rock steady about her waist. Resting for a moment on his strength, she felt safe and secure. She could have floated on that sure, unshakable, unwavering strength forever.

Jace was regarding Bob with something like awe. "Is he always like this?"

His tone, the whole situation, suddenly brought a bubble of irrepressible laughter up into her throat.

"Yes," she said simply and laughed. Bob never cared about his own safety where his inventions were concerned. Ever since she could remember, strange explosions would come from the shack he used as a laboratory, out of which he would stagger covered in grime and grinning widely. His singlemindedness had all the innocence of a two-year-old's curiosity and was as exasperating and as charming.

Jace turned his head to look at her.

Then his eyes changed, darkening. Startled, she looked where he was looking.

Wet, the thin cotton of her shirt was transparent. It clung to her body, to her shoulders and the smooth swell of her breasts. Her nipples showed clearly through the soaked cloth, rosy and hard from the cool sea.

His glance moved over her like a touch, heavy and lingering. Mattie felt a sudden suffocation in her throat, a sudden hot melting deep in the pit of her stomach.

His arm tightened around her waist, turning her to him. Their soaked clothing was no barrier to the heat flaring between them; they might as well have been naked.

She saw his eyes flash with a rueful, reckless laughter, saw his face tighten, his lips part, knew, *knew* that he was going to kiss her. And her hands spread on the soaked cloth of his shirt, closing on the deep warm muscles of his shoulders. Her head fell back, languorous with heat and surrender, feeling his breath warm on her parted lips, wanting his mouth on hers with a violence beyond rational thought, afraid of it with almost equal intensity, not ready yet, not ready at all for a decision such as this.

"For God's sake, are you people all right?" Sam demanded, breathless with the speed with which he had run all the way from the pier.

They jerked around, catching at the rocks for balance.

Sam was regarding Bob with resignation as he crooned over the resurrected *Mako*, oblivious to everything else.

"I should have guessed," he said. Then they were all regarding Bob with that rueful affection, which was where everybody inevitably ended up with Bob.

"Why did you jump in?" Jace asked in Mattie's ear. "You could have been killed. Didn't you think of that?"

"Did you?"

"That's different."

Mattie reared back like a snake about to strike, eyes narrowing dangerously.

"Why the hell is it?"

"Hey. Hey there!" said Sam, but they ignored him.

"I wish you'd get that protective reflex of yours under control, Jace Wyatt!" she said angrily.

"We seem to have the same reflex, Mattie. Let's discuss who'd be more useful."

"You listen to me, Jace," she said between her teeth. "If it's someone I care about, I'm not sitting around with my hands folded, useful or not! I'm going after them come hell or high water and you'd better get that through your head right now!"

There was an odd, arrested, faintly startled look on his face.

"You would, wouldn't you?" he said under his breath.

"Are you all through down there?" Sam asked patiently. "Or are you planning to spend the rest of the day floating around yelling at each other?"

Jace looked up, grinning involuntarily. "Okay, Sam." He turned Mattie gently around to face the rocks. "Grab hold."

Sam reached down, caught Mattie's hands and effortlessly pulled her up onto the rocks, then extended a hand to Jace.

Jace looked back at Bob. "Snap out of it, genius."

Bob stared at him, then up at Sam and Mattie crouched on the rocks. His eyes were a vivid blue, totally unseeing.

"Now we go after the real thing," he said, owl-eyed and innocent.

Mattie groaned. Jace laughed.

"Tomorrow, Bob," said Sam patiently. "At first light. Now will you come outta there?"

Even though they started at first light the next day, getting all the little last minute details done took up half the morning.

"C'mon, c'mon, c'mon," Gramps yelled, pacing restlessly up and down the pier. "Can we get together here?"

Sam hitched a hip on a piling. Mattie, sitting on the concrete wall that ran at right angles to the pier, heard Jace's long quiet stride come down the path from the house. She turned her head to look at him and he stopped beside her. Their glances met, guarded and searching.

"*Marilee*'s set," Bob said, hurrying down the trawler's gangway. His face was taut and his teeth were chattering with nervousness.

Gramps was hardly less tense. "You sure you got all the paperwork done on this craft you want to raise?" he demanded of Bob.

Bob nodded, looked around at all of them. "*Southern Belle,* they called her. She's one-fifty grand's worth of cabin cruiser. Forty-six feet, fiberglass hull, twin diesels. Got a hole stove in her and went down like a stone in seventy-five feet of ocean a half mile south of Looe Key."

"Did you get the rights to her, Bob?" Jace asked and Bob nodded.

"The release form finally came through from the insurance company. They've paid off the owners, so she's all ours if we can bring her up."

Jace nodded and leaned back against the wall, his shoulder brushing Mattie's elbow.

She looked down at the curve of his head, the edge of his contained profile. She wanted to touch him, to put her hand on his shoulder and feel the warmth of his flesh through the soft faded blue workshirt he wore, to feel the strong muscles move under her palm. Just that; nothing more.

Then he turned his head and looked up at her. His eyes were quizzical and half-smiling. Something moved, heavy and obscure, within the black depths and suddenly touching his shoulder was not all she wanted.

"Okay," Gramps was saying. "Sam can take care of things here. Mattie and Jace can run the *Queenfisher*, and you and I'll take the *Marilee*, Bob. That way you can keep an eye on those precious pumps of yours and I can keep an eye on you." He shook his head over the trawler. "She looks a mite discouraged, doesn't she?"

She did. The *Marilee* was as low in the water as Mattie cared to see. Loaded with several fifty-five-gallon drums of Bob's chemicals, the heavy diesel pump, lengths of reinforced hose, scuba tanks, air compressor, tools and torches, she was carrying some seven thousand pounds of extra cargo.

"If she founders," Sam grinned, "you can always raise her with Bob's special gunk."

Mattie smiled involuntarily, then saw the corner of Jace's mouth turn up in amusement. Neither Bob nor Gramps found it in the least funny. They were both experiencing mood swings that ranged from giddy confidence to the glooms and hollow laughter, and Mattie, Jace and Sam had learned not to treat this business lightly in their hearing.

Now that it was time to put the dream to the test, they could not bring themselves to take that final step. It was almost better to contemplate that shining bubble forever out of reach than to risk having it burst in their hands.

Jace levered himself off the wall.

"Mattie and I'll take the lead then," he said and turned and lifted Mattie off her perch. Startled, her hands caught his shoulders for balance, then had a hard time letting go. "What's the forecast like, Sam?"

Sam was grinning. "Good for the next couple of days. But there's a bit of bad weather over near the Leewards and we're into the whirly-girl season now. Might get one screaming up hurricane alley; y'never know."

Jace nodded and looked down at Mattie. Her hands had slid down onto his chest. They lay flattened and spread on the deep muscles there. His face tightened, then he pushed her gently away and stepped back.

"Come on. What are we waiting for?" he said sharply and Bob and Gramps began to move, a little dazed at first, then looking almost relieved to have the decision taken out of their hands.

"You give orders fine," Mattie said under her breath. "You got any problems taking them?"

He glanced down at her, his narrow eyes amused. "I take orders."

"Because there's only one captain on my boat," she said flatly.

"These are your waters, Mattie, and the *Queen*'s your boat."

Mattie was dubious. She had had trouble with fragile male egos before. But Jace took orders without fuss. He turned out to be as good a crew as Sam and that was very good indeed. There was nothing fragile about Jace; his sense of self did not depend on control.

She ran them south past No Name Key and under the fixed bridge between Bahia Honda and Spanish Harbor keys. Then the *Queenfisher* and the overladen *Marilee* were out on the deeps, making the long slow run to Looe.

"Where is Looe Key?" Jace asked and Mattie handed him the chart.

"Nine miles away at about 220 degrees," she said, switching the *Queen* onto automatic pilot and reaching for the coffee Jace had brought up from the galley. "You really don't know these waters, do you?"

"I was raised on the West Coast. San Diego. Don't know Florida so well and nothing about the Keys." He glanced up from the chart, frowning over the slow heave of greasy swell under the *Queen*. "Feels like there might be trouble on the way despite that forecast."

Mattie nodded. "I've already figured out the best way to run if the weather blows up on us."

He smiled faintly. "I expected that. You're a pro, Mattie."

She was pleased. "Thank you."

He bent over the chart again. "Why is it called Looe?"

"It's named after a frigate that went aground there in 1774. Looe's a National Marine Sanctuary, so when we go down don't touch or stand on the coral. It's protected like all other life in the sanctuary."

"All right."

She watched him poring over the chart. He had pulled on an off-white poplin windbreaker over the blue work-shirt left hanging out over his white sailcloth slacks and white deck shoes. The wind blew strands of his black hair across his forehead, flipped the edges of his half-buttoned shirt back and forth over the deep muscles of his throat and chest.

And suddenly she saw what he must have looked like in his teens, absorbed and intent, fooling around on boats over on the West Coast.

"Were you born in San Diego?" she asked and he looked up, amused.

"I was born in Naponee, Nebraska," he said and grinned as she laughed involuntarily in surprise.

"How did a Nebraska farm boy end up in the navy?"

His mouth twisted sardonically. "Mama went back to her folks to have me because as usual Papa was away at sea."

She heard the mockery in his choice of words. "You're one of us then," she said lightly. "The latch-key kids."

"Guess so." He came and sat on the bench beside the console on which she was leaning. "I was a navy brat, had the run of all the bases my dad was posted at. There were a lot of bases. Even when he got himself posted shoreside at San Diego, I was more at home on the base than in the city. I guess it was inevitable I join up."

"Is he still living?"

"No. Heart." He glanced up at her, eyes narrowing wryly, knowing the next question. "My mother left us a few years after his shoreside posting. Went back to Ne-braska. Married again. We keep in touch."

Mattie looked at him in surprise. "She left *after* his posting shoreside?"

He smiled crookedly, watching her. "You're thinking if she were going to she should have left before. She came close. The reason my dad asked for shore duty was that he thought it would keep the marriage together." He looked down at his hands, his mouth twisting fractionally. "Instead it took the heart out of him and the marriage broke up, anyway. That's why I knew better when my turn came."

She glanced at his guarded face. It was a kind of explanation—and another warning.

"What was her name?"

He didn't pretend to misunderstand.

"Ellie."

"You loved her very much."

"I loved her," he said. "But maybe not enough. I couldn't give up the sea for her when she asked me."

"You're shoreside now, Jace," she said gently and his eyes came up to hers, level and cold. "You could go back, pick up the pieces."

He looked down at his hands.

"No."

She looked at his withdrawn face and said nothing. But the question hung in the air and after a while his mouth twisted a little.

"You have your own methods, don't you, Mattie?" Then as her lips parted in instinctive protest, he looked up at her, his eyes narrow and still. "We married young—too young. We both changed. After seven years I was no longer the man she married. Or the man she needed to be married to."

"And you?"

He looked away.

"I'm sorry," she said instantly. "I shouldn't have asked."

He looked back at her and his eyes were cynical slits in his hard, resistive face.

"I learned that nothing lasts. People think it does, but it doesn't. The loving never lasts and no one is capable of going the distance."

There was a small silence. Mattie stared at him and he looked back, level and challenging.

"You're wrong," she whispered, appalled at the depth of the distrust and disbelief suddenly revealed. "Jace, you're very wrong."

"You're too damn young, twenty-four," he said, her age both nickname and gibe. "You believe in people, in permanence. You believe in forever. Nothing's forever, Mattie."

It was the last piece of the puzzle, the key piece, and finally she understood what moved him.

Everything had fallen apart on him—his work, his marriage, his life—and he had no faith in anything anymore. Even the slightest involvement was a monumental risk because he had no faith in it, could not trust it to last, knew only that he was opening himself to inevitable hurt.

She stared at him, seeing the bitterness in his eyes, realizing where and how badly he had been truly scarred, understanding at last the depth of the pain that lay behind all his words and actions. And her heart went out to him, wanting to change that look as she had wanted to erase the scars on his spine.

Everything suddenly fell simply, shiningly, into place.

She reached out very gently and touched his face, her hand sliding delicately from temple to jawline, and up again to cradle the strong curve of his jaw, thumb moving lightly over the flat plane of his cheek, the solid jut of his cheekbone.

He recoiled faintly, glancing down at her hand. She felt the shudder of his breath on the inside of her wrist, then he looked back up at her, his eyes widening, very young in surprise and disbelief.

"Even if nothing lasts, Jace," she whispered, "isn't the moment sweet?"

He drew a harsh breath. His hand shot up to grip her wrist, then hesitated, torn between pulling her caressing fingers away and pressing them to his face. His eyes had darkened, were all stillness and heat.

"Mattie," he said in a harsh whisper almost under his breath. "You don't know what you're saying."

"I know."

He shook his head, his hand tightening unconsciously on her wrist.

"Listen to me. The price is too high."

"The price," she whispered, "is worth it."

"Mattie, haven't you heard a word I've been saying? I'm eight years older than you...."

"So old," she mocked.

"Damn it, yes! I'm a hundred years older than you, twenty-four. I've got one failed marriage behind me and a body that could quit on me any second...."

"That doesn't matter," she whispered.

"It matters! I'm trying to build a future on another man's dreams, trying to make a life for myself in a world I don't know, but that I do know to be unstable. I don't need involvement. Not now. Not with someone like you, someone who believes in permanence, someone who still has stars in her eyes."

"Do you hear me talking about permanence?"

"You're not the type for an affair," he said flatly.

"How do you know? You're running scared," she murmured. "You got burned once and you're terrified to risk anything ever again. Isn't that it, Jace?"

She saw the flash of anger in his eyes.

"Mattie, I've got nothing to give."

"Only yourself," she whispered. "Is that nothing?"

He came to his feet like a tightly wound spring uncoiling and she backed involuntarily from the sudden surge of force in his face. His grip on her wrist jerked her back.

"It's still a game to you," he said between his teeth. "You keep playing with fire and don't even realize that you might get burned. Maybe you should get burned, Mattie. Maybe then you'll think twice."

She saw his eyes above her, a black intensity of suppressed violence, saw teeth set on edge between the beautiful parted lips, a face all hard anger and heat—saw all the storm signals she had missed because of his rigid control.

But she had no fear of him. He was a man capable of violence—and utterly incapable of using that violence on anyone weaker than he. And she smiled and lifted her face to his.

Then his mouth took hers in abrupt explosive demand and all thought deserted her.

She was drowning; she was burning. This was devastating, completely beyond her wildest imaginings, the thunderbolt at the heart of the storm.

His kiss was deliberately brutal, intended to shock her into resistance. But she was far beyond resistance, lost in a sudden, opening world of sensation she had never known before.

The desultory kisses of her occasional dates had prepared her for nothing like this. Desire was a lightning

stroke transforming the landscape of her imaginings—
and nothing would ever be the same again.

Her head fell back; her lips opened to him without a
thought; her body shuddered, turned, nestling into his,
surrendering itself totally to him, reckless and uncaring.

She felt the jolt of his rib cage, the harsh rasp of his
breath.

"Mattie," he said against her mouth, a suffocated
sound like a curse, and she felt the sudden heat of his
skin, the sudden urgency of his body turning full to hers,
pressing her back against the console.

That rigid control of his was shattered, his original
intention forgotten in this tidal wave of passion.

His mouth twisted on hers, gentleness beyond him,
bruising her lips as he pressed deeper, closer, the hard
thrusts of his tongue finding every corner of her mouth,
setting her mouth on fire. She was drowning in sensation, drunk on the feel of him, the taste of him, her
hands dragging with a fierceness that matched his, down
the contours of his face, feeling his cheeks hollow under
her palms as he took her mouth again and again in those
violent, devouring kisses.

His mouth tore itself away, moved across her face, his
breath hot and shuddering against her skin, and, freed,
her lips found the line of his jaw, trailed down the side
of his neck.

"Oh, God, I've wanted this," he muttered, and she
hardly heard him through the dizzying pounding of her
blood in her veins, all sounds hazy, even sight blurred,
nothing left but sensation.

"The way you feel . . ." she whispered, unaware even
of speaking. "I never knew, I never knew. . . ."

Her body was beyond her control, arcing and twisting mindlessly against the firm resilient planes of his chest and stomach. Her hands moved compulsively under the open edges of his shirt to find his naked flesh, to rub up and down the deep muscles of his hair-roughened chest, unconsciously, instinctively, stimulating him, feeling the flat coins of his nipples harden under the friction of her palms.

She heard the harsh gasp of his breath, then his hands tangled in her hair, dragging her head back. Sunlight flashed red through her closed eyelids and the world was all fire.

His mouth raked down her throat. His hands twisted her further backward, dragging her up against his body bent like a bow on hers. Then she felt his mouth working on her breast through the thin cotton of her shirt. And she cried out in shock at the pleasure that shot through her like a stroke of lightning, agonizing and unbearable.

He was suddenly still.

"Mattie, for God's sake!"

Dazed, she saw his face above hers, blocking the light, drawn and gaunt with passion and strain.

"Don't you ever learn? Is that what you want? Is it?"

And his hands caught her hipbones in a painful grip and roughly aligned her pelvis to his. Then his weight came fully upon her, that weight of muscle and bone and taut flesh pressing her hard against the console, that sudden sensual weight of him that was more ruthlessly arousing than his mouth.

Her body arced mindlessly to his. She heard the harsh exhalation of his breath, her own gasp of shock and primitive response.

This was too quick, too urgent, too unknown. The depth of her own response stunned her. She was not ready for this. Her hands found his shoulders, pressed blindly for release.

But he was not ready to let her go yet. He tilted his torso back a little to look into her face and his eyes were all anger and heat and a strange kind of amusement. The movement pressed his hips harder against hers and she shuddered involuntarily, feeling the intensity of his arousal, stunned by the swell of blinding reckless desire that surged through her.

"That's what it is," he said between his teeth. "That's all it is, Mattie. That's all it'll ever be."

And his mouth took hers again in mocking, working kisses. His hands on her wrists pressed her palms harder into his flesh, rubbing them up and down his chest.

"Don't," she muttered through the heavy haze of desire. "Jace, don't."

He laughed harshly against her mouth. Then his hands dropped to the console on either side of her and he levered himself away.

"Gramps's golden child," he said with derision.

She leaned heavily on the console, unable to speak, one hand gripping the cold metal, the other on his chest holding him away, though he made no effort to come closer.

They were both gasping for breath, shuddering with the intensity of the passion beating like a storm on them.

His face was strained with the effort of getting himself back under control, his lips pulled back in a harsh painful line, his eyes black and bitter.

"Yes, I've been burned, Mattie," he said and his voice was dangerous in its very quiet. "And there's nothing easy about it. It hurts. It leaves scars. Yes, I'm scared.

I've been burned too often. I'm tired of being burned. I'm tired of investing myself in things and watching them die on me. I'm tired of caring.''

"Jace . . .''

"I'm not getting involved. Ever again. I don't want to hurt you, but if you keep pushing I will. I'll use you. That's all it would be—using. Because I don't believe in permanence, I don't believe anything has a future and I'm through making empty promises. So stay away from me. Because the next time I won't stop. The next time I won't give a damn about you.''

His words, his tone, were brutal.

But under her hand on his chest holding him away, she could feel the uneven pounding of his heart. And behind the resistive tension of those harsh eyes watching her was a look of strain, of darkness and vulnerability. She could feel the pain behind the still eyes.

Her lips trembled in a shaky smile.

"Jace,'' she whispered, "you wouldn't be saying this if you didn't give a damn about me.''

His lips parted to speak. Then he didn't.

"You keep saying you don't want to be involved,'' she whispered. "But you keep getting involved. You keep putting yourself out on that limb. You say you don't want to care. But you're the most caring man I know, Jace.''

Her hand rose helplessly from his chest, touched his face with still, intent tenderness.

"And I,'' she said softly, "can't help caring for you.''

His hand caught hers in a bruising grip, holding it hard against his face. Then he turned abruptly and left the bridge.

Five

——

Looe ahead,'' Mattie called. Jace raised a hand in acknowledgement.

They were both being carefully impersonal. But every now and then her gaze would rest on him in wondering amazement and he would look back, his face expressionless. Nothing was settled and they both knew it; the tension surged like an electric current in the air between them, crackling and painful.

Jace felt about as stunned as Mattie looked. But not for the same reason. Desire was an old friend and an old enemy; he was wryly aware of his own appetites and long accustomed to controlling them. But there on the bridge he had lost control—and that had never happened to him before.

For half what he had said and done on that bridge Ellie would have cold-shouldered him for a week. Ellie had never looked below the surface of things. Mattie had seen right through him. Mattie had touched his face, looked at him with that infinite tenderness. He was not accustomed to having his own understanding reflected, tendered to him as a gift.

It shook him. They all shook him. They were so trusting, so openly affectionate, indifferent to the possibility of being hurt. And he wasn't even able to tell himself they were naive or foolish. Sam was no fool, and Sam had set the seal of his approval on him clearly enough for even him to see.

He wanted what they offered him—permanence, affection, caring. Wanted it so badly he hurt. He wanted Mattie. Not just sexually; he had found that out on the bridge. Mattie the person—fierce, loyal, caring Mattie who jumped in to fish Bob out of the water at the risk of her own life, and who put her arms out to him on the bridge because she knew he was hurting. He had felt as if he were coming home.

He ached with wanting. But he had learned long ago that wanting was not enough. Wanting had not saved his marriage; wanting would not change the fact that he had no future. If he had not been able to hold on to Ellie with all the advantages of a job he loved and money to burn and a body he could trust, how could he hope to hold onto Mattie, with a future that was based only on Bob's dreams and a body that could give out on him any second?

So you stop it before it even starts. You put the temptation away flatly as something you simply cannot have, and that was all there was to it.

Except this time it wasn't working.

"We'll get the *Marilee* anchored," Gramps said over the CB, "and use the *Queen* to look for the wreck. Tell

Mattie to come pick us up when she's ready. Okay,
Jace?''

"Okay."

He broke out the wet suits and scuba gear while Mattie swung the *Queen* around the *Marilee*, which Bob and
Gramps had anchored in shoal water as close in as they
could get without risking being hard aground in low tide.
It gave him a remote, bitter pleasure to be handling diving gear again, his memory drifting back over the
hundreds of complex and delicate operations he had
worked. Deep-sea work was something he enjoyed.

"You find everything so easy," Mattie had said and
she was right. Nothing he had done since leaving the sub
had required more than the mindless reflex of ingrained
habit.

The fishing was sporadically interesting. Gramps had
hooked him a tarpon and in those first five minutes before it had sounded and dogged it out, the fish had
jumped and shaken and tailwalked spectacularly, feeling like a falling piano on the end of his line. He had felt
that old familiar rush of adrenaline and excitement and
had understood how this could become habit-forming.

But in the end, fishing was only a diversion. It had no
purpose.

"Somewhere around here," said Mattie as they
reached the approximate position of the wreck. "We'll
have to dive to find her."

He and Bob got into the wet suits and went down
while Mattie idled the *Queen* above them.

This is more like it, he thought, feeling at last the old
satisfying tension of purpose as he and Bob quartered
the area, looking for the *Belle*. The salvage was all that
was left and it had to work.

After about an hour's searching they found the *Belle*, lying on a twenty degree list to port, amidst the sea fans and gorgonians and massive brain coral, the hole in her starboard side clearly visible. She was already filmed with new grass and weeds and green slime so that she looked almost part of the reef and the brilliant, multi-colored schools of tropical fish were very much at home all around her.

It was too late in the day to start work on her. They measured the inner spaces and bulkheads, made notes of the interior layout and the location of the hatches, then went up to tell Mattie and Gramps all about it.

"Lots to do," said Bob glumly as they stripped off their gear. "We'll have to fasten plywood over that hole in her side, beef up other places, cut through some of those interior bulkheads to get a free flow of water through all that below-decks area."

"We've got time," Jace said, watching him with affection as he jittered. He had not intended to get involved with any of them, but they were all, Mattie, Bob, Gramps, Sam, winding themselves into him. "We can do it in shifts. We'll make it if the weather holds."

But Bob was on a down cycle, shivering with tension.

"It'll work, Bob," said Mattie reassuringly. "You know it will. It worked on the *Mako*."

"There's a heck of a difference between the *Mako* and the *Belle*," Bob muttered unarguably and kept on jittering.

In the morning they brought the *Marilee* out and anchored her over the wreck and got down to work.

Bob was in and out of the water all the time, regardless of whose shift it was, and Jace kept pace with him, even though Mattie and Gramps protested.

It was a test—a test of how much the salvage could absorb him. It did not take long for him to realize that it was a test that was going to fail.

Cutting through bulkheads, shoring up walls, nailing plywood over the hole in the *Belle*, was all too easy, not even a mild echo of the far more complex salvage-and-demolition operations that had themselves become no more than routine for him. This was no challenge, not even a distraction, merely grueling hard work and a strain on his back.

"What is it?" Mattie asked, putting a hand on his wrist to stop him as he was going back down again.

He shook his head, forced himself to smile, but knew from the worry in her expressive face that he had not succeeded in hiding his bleakness.

It was past noon the next day before Bob was finally satisfied they were ready to bring up the *Belle*.

He and Jace took the huge reinforced hose down and clamped it securely into the new hole they had cut into her damaged side. Then Bob got the old diesel pump going. It belched and stank and hiccuped, then finally settled down to pumping water up over the *Marilee*'s side and down through the big hose into the *Belle*.

Bob's hands shook as he connected smaller hoses from the various drums of chemicals to the main one.

"Right," he said. "That should do it. Gramps, Mattie, keep an eye on those gauges. Jace, keep that hand pump going."

"How long ... ?"

"I don't know," said Bob, biting a knuckle. "Long as it takes, I guess."

He and Jace spelled each other on the hand pump. Mattie and Gramps alternated between watching the gauges and leaning way over *Marilee*'s side to peer into the sea below. Nothing seemed to be happening.

An hour later Bob was leaning over the rail, and all the others were looking worried. None of them liked the feel of the weather. The swell beneath the *Marilee* was far stronger and the wind came in odd irregular hot puffs, like the moist panting of a predator's breath on the back of their necks, an early warning of the storm padding swiftly toward them.

"Bob, maybe we should go down for a look," Mattie suggested and suddenly Gramps gave a yell, shocking her heart right up into her throat so that she nearly strangled.

Coughing, she saw that the hose was standing up out of the water like a snake. A moment later the big cruiser shot up so fast and so close that she threw a wave aboard the *Marilee*, drenching them to the skin and killing the pump.

It was like magic: one moment there was nothing but empty sea and the next there was the *Belle*, riding high and handsome and streaming water from dozens of tiny holes.

Gramps was yelling and stomping and pounding a dazed Bob on the back. Mattie and Jace hung over *Marilee*'s side, shouting. They were all laughing like idiots.

"Minimum sixty thousand return after repair costs and brokerage commission," Bob was muttering, his face fixed in a broad, beaming grin.

Hands on the rail, Jace swung around.

"Let's get out of here. Come on, people! That squall's coming up fast. We won't have a thing to celebrate until we get her back."

He was already unhooking the hose.

"Mattie, take the apparatus apart. Bob, get those drums lashed down. You and Gramps take the lead in the *Marilee*. We'll put the *Belle* between us on short towlines. That way if your tow starts to swing, Mattie can pull her back into line, keep her from riding up your stern if you have to stop down for traffic."

They wasted no time getting rigged for towing. But it was still well past midnight before they got the *Belle* over to the Harkness Boat Yards, and then they had to work her in during a flat squall, in a hard, gray driving rain and a gusting whistling wind.

They had called ahead via the marine operator, so the yards were waiting for them. They shoved the *Belle* into the slings and the boat yard people picked her out of the water and put her on a cradle and ran her along the rails into one of the big sheds, ready for work in the morning.

Then they had to get themselves back home. By the time they had got the *Marilee* and the *Queenfisher* properly moored, the rain was thundering down.

"Now we break out the booze," said Gramps jubilantly. "Shower and change and gather up in the kitchen, people. I'm gonna help Sam whip up a ton of his chili."

"There's a steel barge down off Key Blanca," Bob said dreamily, "that'll come up just like a balloon...."

"Yeah, yeah," said Gramps, steering him toward the house. "Can we talk about it out of the wet?"

"Wet?"

Gramps rolled his eyes. Mattie laughed, looked over at Sam opening the front door to wave them in, ran ahead to tell him all about it.

It was wonderful to stand under the hot shower, feeling her sore muscles ease. A contented tiredness filled her with lazy satisfaction and a ravenous hunger roused as the aroma of Sam's special chili came wafting up from the kitchen.

Coming downstairs, warm and dry once more, she could hear Gramps and Sam talking in the kitchen, and Bob singing off-key and crazy in the shower. The house was alive with laughter and triumph.

At the door to the living room, she stopped abruptly.

Jace was sitting on one of the bar stools and he looked exhausted.

He had changed into jeans, a fresh white shirt and sneakers, but the shirt was pulled out of his belt and left hanging around his hips in an effort to hide the stiffness of his back.

Everything about him from the hunched way he was sitting to the whiteness of the skin around his mouth showed that he was hurting.

As she watched, he took a long swallow from his glass, his eyes screwed shut, then pushed the glass away from him and hunched forward on the bar.

"Jace?"

He started, swinging around a little on the bar stool before he stopped himself with an outstretched foot. Then his guard came back up. He straightened, smiled. But Mattie saw his shoulder blades flex unconsciously as he tried to ease his spine.

"Gramps and Sam are cooking up a storm," he said, his eyes wary.

"So I hear." She came toward him. "Your back's giving you trouble."

A shutter came over his eyes. "I'm fine," he said and turned away from her gaze. There was a thin film of sweat on his forehead, and the tendons of his neck were corded with strain.

"Jace," she said gently. "You're hurting."

He leaned over the bar to reach for a bottle. "Want a drink?"

"No."

"I hate to drink alone. Send Gramps in here." He grinned crookedly at her. "Gramps never passes up a drink."

"Jace," she said firmly.

"No jokes, huh?" He looked around at her over his shoulder, resigned. "All right, Mattie, it hurts. But there's nothing anyone can do about it, so let's forget it, okay?"

"Let me help."

He swayed away from her outstretched hand.

"Mattie, believe me, the last thing my back needs is some well-meaning amateur fooling around with it. Mattie, don't touch me!" he exclaimed almost in panic as she reached for him. "Mattie...Hunh!"

Her hand had pressed firmly into the small of his back.

He arced backward away from it, with an involuntary snarl of pain. Then his breath slowly escaped between his teeth and he slumped forward on the bar. Mattie's hands worked firmly, steadily, in the small of his back.

"Where...did you...learn that?" he asked on a gasp of breath.

"Gramps slipped a disc a couple of years ago," she said quietly. "I was interested, so the physiotherapist showed me a lot more than she needed to."

He leaned further forward on the bar, head hanging, eyes closed in an intensity of relief.

"I thought they told you to take it easy at that hospital," she said tightly.

"You mad?" he murmured.

"Yes, damn it!"

"Bob, Gramps, me. You get mad, you kill us with kindness."

She saw that he was laughing under his breath.

"Oh, shut up," she growled. "You didn't have to push yourself so hard. Why didn't you say something?"

The laughter stopped. His lips tightened into a straight compressed line, their corners pointed. It was a look she knew, a look of anger and frustration.

"I like to keep busy."

There was a lot more to that flat statement than showed on the surface. That look of frustration was telling. The salvage had not worked for him. Mattie had not thought it would.

"Can you take your shirt off?" she asked quietly, anger lost.

He hesitated fractionally, reluctant to have his scars seen. But this was Mattie, for whom one did not have to keep up that illusion of macho perfection, who knew his vulnerabilities and did not despise him for them.

He fumbled with the two buttons holding his shirt together, then shrugged his shoulders to work it off. She helped him with one hand, the other still kneading steadily in the small of his back. Shirt discarded on the floor, he leaned his forehead on his crossed wrists, sighed as her hands worked along his spine.

"It doesn't bother you, does it?" he muttered.

Mattie looked at the ugliness of the scars that cross-hatched the small of his back, the puckered welts and shiny tissue of the explosion, the neater lines of surgery.

"It bothers me," she said quietly and her hand slid over the scars as if trying to wipe them out of existence.

"Not the way I mean."

"Of course not," she said in surprise.

He sighed against his crossed wrists. Of course not, she'd said, as if anything else were completely impossible.

Ellie would have recoiled. He knew that, though he would never tell that to anyone. Ellie would have looked away with a sick face, and then would have tried to pretend the scars did not exist. And then whenever they made love, Ellie's hands would have avoided that part of his body.

Mattie felt the tension in him, saw the strain in the brooding withdrawn face half-hidden against his wrists. She wanted to ask: what is it? She wanted to say: I love you, let me help. But that averted face stopped all words, stillborn on her tongue.

So she concentrated on what she could do to help.

She felt his muscles ease under her hands as she worked on him, found herself falling into a haze of her own, involving touch and scent and sight. He was beautiful under her hands, all smooth skin and deep taut muscle, the scars in no way marring the finely made shape of him. Her hands clung to the smooth swells and hollows of his back, the long indent of his spine, the deep warm flesh and rapidly heating skin.

"Mattie," he said abruptly in a suffocated voice. "Mattie, take your hands away."

"What?" she murmured, lost in that sensual haze.

"Mattie!"

She gasped as he swung suddenly around on the stool. His hands caught her wrists, jerking her hands from him, and she staggered, thrown off balance by his thigh striking her as he turned. The heels of his hands jolted on her upraised forearms, bracing her.

Then everything seemed to stop.

She realized they were both breathing very fast, only then became aware of her own arousal.

"Mattie, don't you ever think of consequences?" he asked in exasperation.

"Always," she said quietly and met his dangerous gaze without wavering. Smiling faintly, she surrendered her wrists trustingly to the tight but careful grip of his hands.

For a moment there was absolute silence. She could feel the beating tension in the air, painful and exhilarating. She was committed now beyond recall, all doubts gone, knowing with utter surety that this was the man she loved, that she would never stop loving this man, whatever the price, whatever the cost.

His eyes changed, darkening, faintly strained at the corners. His hand released one wrist, came up slowly as if he could not help himself, to brush the heavy wave of her hair back from her face, fingertips sliding delicately over the plane of her temple, the contours of her face.

"I wish I had met you ten years ago," he said almost under his breath.

"When your heart was young and gay?" she murmured, eyes half-shut under that sensitive, caressive touch, that look of still, brooding wistfulness in his face.

"When I still had faith."

"Some things don't have to change, Jace."

"You're so sure of that. What do you know, twenty-four?"

"I know you, Jace," she said simply. "And you know me. Ever since that first day on the pier."

A little muscle jumped betrayingly beside the corner of his mouth.

"We don't change, you or I," she whispered.

"You're wrong," he said.

She laid her free hand on the smooth curve of his shoulder, ran her fingers along his collarbone to the hollow of his throat, then down to his chest, to rake lightly through the rough scattering of hair. She felt his body tighten and clench, heard the harsh catch of his breath. Under her palm flattened on his chest she could feel the racing thud of his heart.

His hand shot up, caught her wrist, dragged her hand away.

"Stop it, Mattie."

She drew a deep breath, took the biggest gamble she had ever taken in her life.

"I want you, Jace."

"Don't say that," he muttered.

"I think I love you."

His grip clenched painfully on her wrist. "Don't, Mattie!"

"I think you need to hear it."

His face was absolutely still. He was hardly breathing. Neither was she. She could feel the sudden urge of force in the air, the sudden pulsing violence of blood heat and urgency.

"All right, Mattie," he said harshly. "Let's talk about need. Let's talk about price."

The note of raw anger in his voice held her suddenly still, staring at him.

"All those pretty words," he said derisively. "I've said them; I've had them said to me. They don't mean a thing to me anymore. I've been trapped by pretty words before. There's always a price to them."

"There's no price!" she exclaimed, appalled.

"You're asking me to lay myself on the line; that's the price! I've done that before. I've done that over and over, and every time I've come up empty. I'm not laying myself on the line ever again!''

"Jace," she whispered, "I'm not asking anything I'm not offering."

"I know," he said on a fierce, harsh breath. "I know. That's why I'm all wrong for you. I'd cheat you of that, Mattie. That's something I don't have to give."

He looked down at her wrists in the hard grip of his fingers, realized he might be hurting her and slackened his hold immediately till she hardly felt the pressure of his hands. But the light touch was inflexible.

"You offer so much," he said. "And, God, I want it! I want it." His eyes came up to hers, black and burning. "But what's given can be taken away again. Some small quarrel, separation, a difference of opinion, time itself—and then everything that went before, all the days and months and years, all the *nights*," he said with sudden bitter violence, "all that means nothing! And I'm back in the cold again."

She saw the raw pain in his eyes, wanted to put her arms around him, could not because of his grip on her wrists holding her away.

"Never again," he said on a harsh breath.

"So instead you'll live in the cold forever?" she asked gently.

"Hope's more cruel than the cold. Hope's a knife in the gut. I'd rather have nothing at all than go through that again. Wanting and being afraid of losing, fear like an animal in your gut clawing at you all the time, hoping it won't happen, knowing it will.... No!" he said violently. "I've been there too many times."

He looked up at her. His face was strained, so set it might have been carved out of stone.

"I can't trust in anybody's loyalty anymore, Mattie. I'm not about to make an exception for you."

She was very still, her gaze searching his rigid face.

"Trust," she said slowly. "That's the operative word, isn't it, Jace? You can't trust me. You can't trust anybody. It doesn't matter what we do, how much we care for you, you still won't take that chance, will you?"

He drew a harsh, ragged breath.

"Mattie, I can't keep cutting myself up over lost causes. If I could find one thing that remained stable, if I could find one thing I could believe in, then maybe I could take a chance on this. But I can't. I can't."

"You could try believing in me," she said quietly.

His face hardened.

"All right," she said and kept her voice steady only by a fierce effort of will. "I'm sorry. You keep talking of price. If there's a price to be paid, I'm willing to pay it. I'd never have asked it of you. I'm naive enough to think loving is worth taking a chance on, whatever the cost."

She turned away, then found herself jerked to a stop by his fingers tightening around her wrists. She looked back and saw something intense and painful move in his strained face, saw words trembling on his taut parted lips.

Then his gaze dropped. He let her go.

Say **Yes** to romance

AND YOU'LL GET:

- **4 FREE BOOKS**
- **A FREE BRACELET WATCH AND**
- **A FREE SURPRISE GIFT**

**NO RISK •
NO OBLIGATION TO BUY •
NO STRINGS • NO KIDDING**

EXCITING DETAILS INSIDE ➔

Say YES to free gifts worth over $20.00

Say YES to a rendezvous with romance and you'll get 4 classic love stories—FREE! You'll get an attractive bracelet watch—FREE! And you'll get a delightful surprise—FREE! These gifts carry a value of over $20.00—but you can have them without spending even a penny!

MONEY-SAVING HOME DELIVERY

Say YES to Silhouette and you'll enjoy the convenience of previewing 6 brand-new Desire®books delivered right to your home every month before they appear in stores. Each book is yours for only $2.24*—a savings of 26¢ off the cover price plus only 69¢ postage and handling for the entire shipment. If you're not completely satisfied, you can cancel at any time, for any reason, just by sending us a note or a shipping statement marked "cancel" or by returning any unopened shipment to us at our cost.

SPECIAL EXTRAS—FREE!

When you join the Silhouette Reader Service,™ you'll get our monthly newsletter, packed with news of your favourite authors and upcoming books—FREE! You'll also get additional free gifts from time to time as a token of our appreciation for being a home subscriber.

Say YES to a Silhouette love affair. Complete, detach and mail your Free Offer Card today!

* In the future, prices and terms may change, but you always have the opportunity to cancel your subscription.

FREE—BRACELET WATCH

You'll love your elegant bracelet watch. This classic LCD quartz watch is a perfect expression of your style and good taste—and it's yours free as an added thanks for giving our Reader Service a try!

SILHOUETTE BOOKS®

FREE OFFER CARD

4 FREE BOOKS

FREE BRACELET WATCH

FREE SURPRISE BONUS

Place YES sticker here

CONVENIENT HOME DELIVERY

LOW MEMBERS-ONLY PRICES

FREE FACT-FILLED NEWSLETTER

Please send me 4 Silhouette Desire® novels, free, along with my free bracelet watch and free surprise gift. I wish to receive all the benefits of the Silhouette Reader Service™ as explained on the opposite page.

326 CIS 814X
(C-S-D-08/89)

Name _____
(PLEASE PRINT)

Address _____Apt. _____

City _____

Province _____Postal Code _____

Offer limited to one per household and not valid to current Silhouette Desire subscribers. All orders subject to approval.

PRINTED IN U.S.A.

YOUR "NO RISK GUARANTEE"
★ There's no obligation to buy, and the free books and gifts are yours to keep forever.
★ You receive books before they're available in stores.
★ You may end your subscription anytime—just write and let us know or return any
  unopened shipment to us at our cost.

If offer card is missing write to:
"Silhouette Reader Service", P.O. Box 609, Fort Erie, Ontario, L2A 5X3

Business Reply Mail
No Postage Stamp
Necessary if Mailed
in Canada

Postage will be paid by

Silhouette Reader Service™
P.O. Box 609
Fort Erie, Ontario
L2A 9Z9

RUSH! FREE GIFTS DEPT.

Canada Post
Postes Canada
125

Six

So you let it go, and you dealt with the things that came in its place, and you tried to make something for yourself out of them.

The old lesson painfully learned. But this time it didn't seem to do any good.

Mattie stepped back, stepped away, let it all go. That crackle of electricity, that charged awareness, she let it ground in her, dissipate itself in her stillness as if it had never been.

It hurt. More than she had thought it would. That interaction between them, wordless and unacknowledged as it had been, had become essential to her. She felt empty without it.

Tomorrow, she told herself, tomorrow she would get used to this. That worked—putting it off day to day.

It helped that he was away most of the time, working with Bob and Sam in the boat yards to put the *Belle* back

into shape. It helped that without Sam she had to
scramble to run her charters alone; that kept her busy,
kept her from thinking.

She made no attempt to avoid him. Her pride would
not let her do that. She met his gaze with level directness. She spoke to him gravely and with courtesy. But all
the while her eyes were shuttered by the steel walls that
were her defence against the world, her glance was cool
and withdrawn and empty.

He looked back as directly, as expressionlessly, but
something moved, dangerous and angry behind the
narrow slits of his eyes.

She was careful not to touch him. She set a plate or
glass down in front of him rather than handing it to him,
withdrew her fingers before he reached for the object.
When she passed him a piece of equipment on the pier,
she was careful to avoid brushing his fingers.

Once when she did that, he caught her hand, fingers
closing over hers in a bruising grip that for once was
forgetful of its own strength. Startled, she leaned on the
rail of the *Queen*, staring at him. He looked up at her,
the crease between his brows stressed and his eyes black
with suppressed anger and frustration. She said nothing, did nothing, simply leaned on the rail, looking
gravely at him.

After a moment he let her go.

Mattie was relieved. She knew how vulnerable she was
to him, knew she had neither pride nor willpower where
he was concerned.

He watched her. Even with her back turned to him,
she could feel his gaze following her, heavy and brooding. She felt it like a touch on her skin, a weight dragging on her, rejecting and demanding at the same time.

"How long till the *Belle*'s in shape?" Gramps asked.

Sam shrugged. "Not long. We've made a lot of head-way these past three weeks. Bob and Jace have been killing themselves on her."

Bent over the account books she had spread out over the dining-room table, Mattie looked up at the men sprawled in various attitudes of exhaustion around the living room.

Jace turned his head suddenly and looked at her. Their glances met and held. His eyes were brooding and depthless. She was lost. She was not even aware of the passage of time, only of that silken, passionate look that reverberated through her like soft thunder.

"Jace?"

Jace looked around at Gramps with a start. "Sorry."

"That barge off Key Blanca. Can we go after it?"

"Not until we sell the *Belle*. It'll take more than we have right now to buy all the supplies Bob needs."

"Maybe we don't have to wait," Gramps said thoughtfully. "Maybe there's a way to float a line of credit so's we can go after that barge right now."

"The paperwork's almost done. Only that declaration left for the insurance company in Miami and we'll have the release."

"Miami," Gramps muttered. "Yeah, I know a couple of people up there might give us a loan. I could look into it tomorrow, maybe sign those insurance papers while I'm at it. Can someone give me a ride down to the airport tomorrow?"

Jace got restlessly to his feet. "I can. I'm seeing Len Daviot along that way."

"Thanks." Gramps started to heave himself to his feet. "How about some coffee?"

"I'll get it, Gramps," Mattie called from the kitchen where she was refreshing her own cup. "Anyone else want one?"

When there was no answer she put her head around the door, then laughed. Bob was fast asleep on the couch and Sam's head was nodding.

Gramps grinned at her. "No stamina."

She grinned back. "Not like you, huh, Gramps?"

Her laughter died as Jace came into the kitchen from the hallway. For a moment their glances met, then she looked away quickly.

He crossed the kitchen to refill his mug from the percolator on the counter. Mattie, who had been heading that way, changed tack abruptly.

"I could have brought that in for you," she said awkwardly, opening a cabinet on the other side of the room.

"I've got even more stamina than Gramps," he said with that quick, brief smile.

Three weeks ago she would have made some laughing rejoinder. Now it took an effort even to smile. She did, but it was a stiff meaningless lift of the corners of her mouth, and her head was bent and her gaze on the coffee cup she had taken down from the shelf.

She was waiting for him to move away from the percolator. He cast her a quick glance, then walked away to lean against the kitchen table, giving her room. They were reduced to that now, these automatic courtesies. But his eyes watched her as she filled the coffee cups and she could not meet them because just that jerked the tightly wound spring of tension between them one notch closer to the breaking point.

Sam was on his feet when she brought the tray into the living room.

"I'm off to bed," he said, yawning, and ambled toward the hall. "Barometer's falling, Gramps," he said, tapping it as he went by. "Maybe you better wait awhile for that trip to Miami."

"The weather will hold," Gramps said confidently. "Feel it in my bones."

Gramps's bones never lied. The weather held when Jace drove him down to the airport Monday morning. But by the time Mattie got back from her afternoon charter, it had deteriorated into a squall that threatened to grow into something worse.

"Need a ride home, Kev?" she yelled over the wind at the teenager who had been helping her with the charter.

"Yeah, thanks, Mattie. Thanks again," he said as she handed him his pay. "Will you need me again tomorrow?"

"Not if this keeps up."

"My dad says we're due for a big one. Hurricane, maybe," he said hopefully.

Mattie grinned involuntarily. "Bite your tongue."

By the time she dropped him at his house, the light had gone and the rain was coming down so hard that even with the windshield wipers working overtime she could hardly see past the hood of the car.

She pulled up in front of the house with a sigh of relief, pulled her slicker over her head and dashed through the rain to the door.

The place was dark and empty. Mattie snapped on the hall light and looked around in surprise.

"Hey!" she called. "Anybody home?"

"In the kitchen," Jace called back.

She stopped abruptly in the doorway, seeing that he was alone.

"Where is everybody?"

"Gramps is in Miami by now. Bob called, said he and Sam are staying over at a friend's house till the storm blows over. Someone called Danny."

"Danny Norton, yes," Mattie said absently. She was wondering whether they could manage to get through an evening alone together.

"Bob doesn't want to lose even one day working on the *Belle*."

She nodded. "Sell the *Belle*, we can bring up the barge. Sell the barge, we'll be in the black forever, give you a return on that investment, Jace."

"Yes," he said without much interest. It was Bob's dream not his, and he didn't really care about the money.

She watched him for a moment as he piled the makings for a salad on the chopping block. He was wearing tan cords and a coffee-brown tailored shirt open as usual halfway down his chest, cuffs unbuttoned and flapping around his strong wrists. It hurt her to look at him.

Aware of her gaze, he looked up.

"Where have you been?" she asked quickly, gesturing at his clothes. "Surely not just to the airport."

"Len Daviot wanted some help buying himself a boat. Ordered himself a yacht big enough to be called a ship."

"Now if he could only learn to sail it right." She looked away from his gaze. "What's cooking?"

"Chili. That's the only thing I can make. That or wieners and beans. You'd better get changed. You're soaked."

She nodded. She was wet and salt-sticky and her jeans and cotton shirt were clinging uncomfortably to her.

Once upstairs she lingered, nervous to return. She spent an unnecessary amount of time showering and dressing, and finally came reluctantly down, warm and dry and comfortable in an old tank top and wrap-around skirt, bare feet thrust into sandals.

Jace held a lettuce leaf out to her as she passed him. "What does this need?"

She took it carefully, avoiding the touch of his fingers, bit into it, grimaced.

"Vinegar."

"Vinegar." He reached for the bottle.

They were both being very careful, conscious of their isolation in the house.

They kept the conversation neutral as they set the table, then sat down to eat. She was aware of his brooding glance on her face, but never met his eyes. Lifting her gaze no higher than his mouth, she saw with surprise that it was set and the skin around it a little white.

Neither of them had much appetite.

She felt the tension in the room, worse now than it had ever been, wound tight with three weeks of unspoken anger and frustration, and refused to let it affect her. She talked, smiled, with teeth-gritted determination kept up the pretence that they were no more than casual acquaintances accidentally thrown together.

And all the while she found her gaze lingering compulsively on his hands as he broke apart a piece of bread, or on his strong forearms through his flapping sleeves, or on the beautiful line of his body when he leaned back from the table, or on the curve of his throat in the open collar of his shirt. It was hard not to think of the way he had felt under her hands. It was hard not to feel.

She wove stillness like a shield around her, was startled when he suddenly threw down the cheese knife with a clatter onto the table.

"Mattie, come back."

Her lips parted on a startled breath. "What?"

His hand closed over hers, gripping it painfully hard.

"Don't shut me out!"

"Jace..."

"Look at me."

Her lips trembled, then she looked up at him, her gaze blank and empty, her eyelids strained with effort.

"No," he said tightly. "*Look* at me."

"Jace," she whispered despairingly, "You can't have it both ways. I'm not made like that."

They looked at each other with tense, still faces.

"We can't go on like this," he said.

She said nothing, but the shudder of her breath in her mouth was answer enough.

He jerked to his feet, moved away violently across the room.

"I never meant to hurt you," he said between his teeth.

She had forgotten that for him as for her the protective instinct came first, that he was as vulnerable to her pain as she was to his.

"I don't want you to pay a price," she whispered.

He came back swiftly, went down on one knee beside her. His hand gripped her upper arm, drawing her sideways to him. His face was all harsh gaunt angles, his eyes narrow and dark with strain. And all she could think of was how beautiful that face was, upturned and vulnerable to her.

"I don't care about the price," he said between his teeth. "I never did. I said that to push you away and it worked. You threw that switch in your head and that's what I wanted. Only now it's like I've lost a limb. Whatever's between us, I need it. I need it like I need breath."

That was the way she felt. Her eyes widened, opened softly, helplessly, to him. Her hand lifted trembling to his face, hesitated a fraction of an inch from his skin.

"Don't look at me like that," he said harshly and she laughed helplessly under her breath.

"Jace, I can't help it. It's all or nothing for me. I never could do things halfway."

She saw his lips pull back tightly in a grimace of pain.

"Listen to me," he said, his voice gritty with intensity. "Listen. A girl's entitled to hear 'I love you' from her first man, whether it's true or not. But I can't say that to you, Mattie. I won't. All those lying-on-top-of-a-woman words—I won't say them. They're a trap I won't be caught in again."

She laid her palm with infinite tenderness along the side of his face, hearing not the words but the pain behind the words. He shuddered under her touch and his lids lifted and his eyes were all heat and hunger, and she didn't care about anything as long as that look was in his eyes.

"I don't need the words," she whispered. "And if there's a trap, it's one that you're creating. You come and go as you please. I won't hold you. There are no strings. If you want to let it go, walk away, Jace."

"I can't let it go," he said on a harsh breath, an angry despairing sound. "I can't."

He had pulled her down so that her temple rested against his, their breaths ragged against each other's faces.

"Then don't," she murmured. "I don't care about the future. Whether this lasts or not, that's not important. I want you to love me. I want you to let me love you."

"Don't."

"For a month, or a week, or a day, I don't care...."

His mouth stopped her words, violent and despairing on hers. He rose abruptly without breaking their mouths apart, hauling her to her feet, crushing the length of her body painfully hard against him.

Her whole body arced to his; her arms closed tightly around him.

His hands dragged across the delicate bones of her face, forced her head back so that his mouth could slide down the exposed curve of her throat. Her breath left her with a jolt and her hands caught his head, sinking into the thick soft hair, holding his mouth to her throat. Her body strained against his and he shuddered against her.

"You've only yourself to blame, damn you," he said between his teeth. "I've tried to do the right thing. God knows I've tried, Mattie."

"*This* is right," she murmured blindly, and her hands found his shoulders, clung to them, her whole body yielding to his, surrendering itself to him.

Their mouths met, met again in intense, urgent, demanding kisses. His hands moved over her body, taking possession of it, and she gasped against his mouth, sinking against him, weak with pleasure, all her bones gone to water.

He thrust her abruptly away. "Damn it, I'm not going to make love to you on the dining-room floor."

Her breath rushed from her in a little shaky laugh.

"My room's the third one down the hall," she murmured and her eyes were heavy and languorous and the hot color moved in her face. "The bed's turned down and . . ."

"You thought of this," he muttered against her temple.

"I thought of it...." she whispered and pressed her face into the hollow of his shoulder, felt his skin hot under the cool, crisp cotton of his shirt.

"So have I. Too damn long."

He picked her up in one quick swoop and her hands found his shoulders, clung to them as he swept her dizzyingly across the living room and up the stairs. Halfway up, he kissed her bruisingly hard.

"You like this, don't you? It appeals to the romantic in you."

She wrapped her arms around his head, smiled into the glittering, dangerous eyes.

"I like it. So do you."

He laughed under his breath, hit the light switch with his elbow.

Then she was dropped into the middle of the bed and without pause his weight was on her from breast to feet, crushing her down into the mattress. And she cried out involuntarily against his face from the delight of it.

His arms and his shoulders and bent head formed a cave around her head; his hands were twisted in her hair; his taut dangerous face filled her vision.

"You know me too well," he muttered and his voice was harsh and angry.

"You breathe and I feel it," she whispered.

"Damn you, I've been wanting this since that first day on the pier." His open mouth moved across her face, his breath shuddering against her skin, and her eyes closed, helpless and heavy, her arms clenched across his back. "Can't sleep, can't think, wanting you. I've always been a rational man, always been in control. This is irrational; this is all wrong, and I have no control."

"You resent it."

"Yes," he said harshly. "Do you, Mattie?"

"No," she murmured. "I know why I want you, Jace. Ever since that first day on the pier I knew. It's a shock I've been prepared for."

"How far are you prepared? Are you protected, Mattie?"

She smiled at that taut face above her. "I told you, Jace—no strings."

He made a harsh sound in his throat and his fingers entwined in her hair, holding her head still for the bruising intensity of his mouth. She lost herself in the salt-sweet taste of his mouth, hands clenching on the fabric of his shirt, her world telescoping dizzyingly downward only to the taste and scent and drugging, inflaming feel of him.

His mouth twisted slowly on hers, devouring her, and the feeling of the kiss changed with every small movement, every shift of angle, until his tongue had found every corner of her mouth, settled into a hot deep thrusting rhythm that echoed the deepening pulse of heat between them.

She could not keep still. Her hands rubbed up and down his back, across the fine muscles. Her body writhed against his, then she moaned into his mouth because he, too, had begun to move, the length of his strong supple body rubbing in slow sensual cat stretches along the length of hers.

He tore his mouth away. For a moment she saw his face above her, drawn and gaunt with passion, beautiful lips parted on a panting breath, eyes all dark fire.

Then he was dragging her tank top up from her waist, pulling it over her head, off her arms, flinging it away.

"Jace!" she gasped, then cried out with startled pleasure as his hands pressed her shoulders back and his mouth found her naked breasts. Her whole body arced blindly to his mouth; she was crying out in soft helpless breathless gasps with the shock and the delight of it.

His hands were moving over her, calloused palms rough and unbearably stimulating on her skin, gripping and kneading. And her body began to writhe helplessly, uncontrollably, against him, arcing to the pull of his mouth, the rasp of his hands on her skin.

"Your shirt, your shirt..." she muttered, trying to unbutton it, hungry for the feel of his skin against hers, her hands unsteady and clumsy with the dizzying pounding of the blood in her veins.

He twisted, tearing the shirt off, throwing it away. Her breath rushed out between her teeth at the feel of his hair-roughened chest against her sensitized breasts. She saw his eyes burning and intense above her, then his mouth was on hers in hot deep violent kisses.

She slid her hands over his body, gripping and caressing the strong bones and deep muscle, drunk on the feel of him.

"Mattie," he muttered against her mouth. "I want this to be right for you. If you keep doing that..."

But she could not stop. She needed to touch him with a hunger beyond will. She felt him shudder and gasp against her as she was shuddering, felt his pleasure, wanted to give him pleasure with an intensity that burned every other thought from her mind.

He twisted away from her, his mouth still on hers. She felt him dragging off the rest of his clothes, felt his hands on her feet, stripping off her sandals, at the tie of her skirt, breaking it with one jerk of his hands. Then he was folding the skirt back on either side of her, and she fell apart in agonizing delight as his mouth found her navel, then the hollow of her hipbone, then the length of her inner thigh as he slid the rest of her clothing from her.

Her hands dragged on his shoulders to bring his mouth to hers, his weight upon her.

"Jace. Jace. I need.... I need...."

"Not yet," he muttered, and his weight came completely upon her and she gasped in delight and an agony of frustrated desire, needing him within her, dying for him even while in his arms. "Not yet, Mattie."

She had never realized before how the body could be used as an instrument of the most terrible pleasure. He used his like that, hands and mouth and teeth and sweat-slick body driving her over the edge of madness until she was writhing uncontrollably under him, head turning feverishly on the pillow, hands sliding imperatively over his body, feeling him jerk under the touch as she was writhing under his.

He bit her shoulder deliberately and she felt the tiny sting of his teeth as unbearable stimulation.

Then his hands slid along the inside of her thighs and she felt his weight shift and met the blind deep surge of his body with a moan of intense satisfaction, not pain.

He stilled, deep within her, and she opened her dazed eyes to see his face above hers, gaunt with strain, jaw clenched with control.

"Am I hurting you?" he asked, his body moving in tight, tiny, involuntary circles against her, inflaming both of them. "Mattie, shall I stop?"

She knew he would even now, whatever it cost him, if she said so. Knew she would come apart in agony if he did.

"Don't stop," she gasped. "Oh, Jace, don't stop!"

And her body surged against his, clenched around him.

She heard the grunt of his breath as his control broke. Then his mouth took hers and his body drove forward against hers. He tore his mouth away and she saw his head go back, the tendons of his throat corded with strain, saw his eyes close with his own pleasure, his lips part on a pant of breath. Then there was nothing but the straining thrusting rhythm of his body and the unbearable tension building within her, as if she were reduced only to a network of charged silver wires, tautening unbearably to breaking point.

Her nails raked his back, her body writhed and clenched on him, eyes blind, lost to everything but sensation.

"Yes, like that, yes," he said, his voice tightened and gritty with effort.

She was crying out in wordless sounds, clinging to him as the one stable point in this fire-shot blackness, in this agony of unbearable pleasure, nothing left but him and the violence of his body shaking hers, driving her ruthlessly up the spiraling paths of pleasure to that choking, urgent, unendurable climax. She felt herself splinter into a million glittering fragments, heard at the same moment the harsh gasp of his breath as his body went rigid and shuddered in convulsive release against her.

He lay heavy upon her, his face thrust into the hollow of her shoulder, and dreamily, hazily, lost in profound unbelievable satisfaction, she kissed his hair and his temple and his closed eyes.

Then his lips moved against her shoulder, his eyes flickered open, he began to gather himself.

"No, don't go," she whispered, her arms winding tight around him, holding him to her. "Stay with me, stay in me...."

She heard the shuddering rasp of his breath.

"I don't want to hurt you," he murmured against her face. "I'm too heavy...."

"No. I want your weight. I want all your weight."

Her body was still shuddering with small residual clampings. She heard the catch of his breath, then his face pressed hard against hers and he took part of his weight on his elbows.

"Mattie," he whispered. "Mattie, you're beautiful."

"Oh, Jace." Her breath shook in her mouth. "Is it always like this?"

"Almost never," he murmured dimly. "Never. Never before for me like this."

Her eyes came open wide. He could see himself reflected in the darkness of her pupils, as if there were nothing in her awareness but him, felt her surrendered to him in a totality of giving that shook the heart in him.

"How can something so wrong feel so right?" he muttered.

Her hands stroked his face with still wonder, fingertips sliding across bone and hollow, cherishing him, and involuntarily he turned his face into her touch.

"Because it is right," she whispered. "It couldn't be more right."

He pressed against her, needing to lose himself in her, forget thought, forget reality. His movements drew a gasp from her and the reflexive pulse of her hips. They were still so violently sensitized to each other that passion came like a stroke of lightning, with no more than touch of hand on skin, the brush of open mouths. He felt himself hardening, saw her eyes widen at the sudden swelling within her.

Then her arms came up around him and the world was lost.

Seven

He lay listening to the storm beating against the windows, reluctant to move. His inner clock told him it was about ten in the morning, but there was no need for them to get up, no duties that were not on hold till the storm blew over. And he was filled with a vast, all-pervading contentment, a bittersweet aching that made him unwilling to give up this moment, to leave the warmth of the bed and their bodies surrendered to each other and her slender supple arms fast around him.

It had been a night of small entangled sleeps and awakenings, of love made in bed, in the shower, back in bed again.

He tucked his chin down and kissed the top of her head. Between them, they had ended up arranging her on top of him, so distributed that she seemed to have no weight at all. Her honey-gold head was tucked under the angle of his jaw, her hands under him and hooked back over his shoulders, her hips astraddle his right thigh, a light sweet whispery weight.

He stroked the smooth contours of her back over and over again with slow, dreaming pleasure, palm running from the sharp delicacy of her shoulder blades down the supple spine to the deep curve of her waist where she was as narrow as a child, then to the unexpectedly rich swell of her hips.

Every now and then as he brought his hand sliding back up, he would flatten it more strongly against the small of her back, for the sheer pleasure of feeling the little reflexive pulse of her hips, the small clenching of her fingers on his shoulders, the quick catch and slow exhalation of her breath warm against his throat. They were still so sensitized to each other that it would take little more than that to rouse them once again to that ever-new, ever-unwearied heat and hunger.

Mattie gave a deep sigh of contentment against the hollow of his throat. He felt her lips move against his skin, tightened his arms around her.

"You must be uncomfortable," she murmured. "Should I move?"

"No. I'm comfortable. I'm so comfortable I may not move for a year." He rubbed the underside of his jaw over the top of her silky head. "Who'd have thought I'd ever be thankful for a storm?"

She laughed, raised her head, hitched herself up so that she was lying on his chest, propping herself up by her elbows on either side of his head, her hair falling like a silky golden curtain around both their faces.

"I feel as if the storm's been in here, not out there," she murmured.

She looked down at him through the clinging cobweb strands of her hair, shaking her head a little to clear them out of her face. Her eyes were languid and smiling and soft with tender laughter.

"Now what does that mean?" He stroked her hair carefully out of her face, fingers delicate on the fragile curves and contours under his hand.

"That means I've never been so shook up, turned inside out, driven right out of my mind." She brushed her lips back and forth over his, with the tip of her tongue explored the corner of his mouth. "I had no idea you were such a stud."

Startled and delighted, he laughed involuntarily. "Blame it on all those months in the hospital."

"Oh, I see." She bit his lower lip deliberately. "It wasn't me at all then. You were just making up for lost time, is that it?"

"Of course." He pulled her head down, kissed her bruisingly hard, and felt intense pleasure as her body trembled and melted upon him. "Mattie. Mattie. You're a miracle."

"I thought you weren't going to say them," she murmured mockingly.

"What?"

"All those lying-on-top-of-a-woman words."

He laughed involuntarily. "You're not going to let me forget that, are you?"

"No," she said and kissed him, smiling.

His hands tightened on her head, feeling the bones delicate in his grip, the entire fragility of her surrendered so trustingly to him. And a deep swell of despairing, protective tenderness surged up in him. He wanted to keep her safe, keep her protected forever—even from him.

"I keep feeling I've cheated you," he muttered.

She rubbed one finger gently over the crease between his brows, trying to erase it. "How?"

"You've got your whole life ahead of you and I've used up most of mine. Seen too much, done too much, been disappointed too often. The way you see things, Mattie, it's right. It's right to see things without cynicism or defeat or despair. I don't want the way I see things to rub off on you."

She bent and kissed his eyes shut with intent tenderness and he lay still, almost afraid to move for fear of spoiling this moment, feeling the light sweet movement of her lips on his eyelids and suddenly, ridiculously, hurting from the very sweetness of it.

"Oh, God, Mattie, I don't want to hurt you."

"Then don't," she said simply, but he knew it was not that simple. Nothing was that simple.

She felt his arms tighten bruisingly hard on her. His eyes came open and the storm was in them, had never really left, that black confusion of anger and doubt and yearning.

"Stop thinking," she whispered. "Stop thinking, Jace. Just let it happen."

"I could sink into you for a thousand years," he muttered. "Wind you around me like a shield against the world. Forget tomorrow, forget everything but you. I wish I could, Mattie."

"Try, Jace," she whispered, then lost all her breath as his mouth took hers with sudden violence.

The storm lasted three days and they spent most of the time making love.

"You're beautiful; did you know that?" she murmured, watching him as he lay on his stomach in a tangle of sheets, propped up on his elbows. The one lamp, bright now that night had fallen again, cast patterns of gold and black along the supple muscles of his back.

He was both embarrassed and pleased, didn't know where to look.

"Not exactly handsome, but beautiful," she amended.

He grinned crookedly. "That's the way I've always thought of myself," he said, mocking, and she laughed and kissed his shoulder. He rubbed the side of his face against hers, smiling.

"Why do men get so embarrassed if you say something like that?"

"Because they'd prefer a little something about character."

"Oh," she teased. "You haven't got anything like that at all. You're just a pretty face."

He started to laugh. "You win. Hey, where are you going?"

Her mouth was following her hands down his back, exploring the supple swells of muscle. She bit his shoulder blade lightly and he shivered.

"Practicing some of your lessons," she murmured.

"Boy, for a novice you sure took a quantum leap into absolute mastery in no time at all."

Her mouth slid down his spine, smiling. "Original sin."

"Getting more original by the second."

She felt him tense as her hand reached the scars at the small of his back.

"Am I hurting you?" she asked, fingers lying still on the scars.

"No," he said in a suffocated voice. "Mattie..."

She bent and kissed the scars, felt his body jerk in shock.

"You'll just have to get used to the idea that there's nothing about you that I don't find beautiful, Jace Wyatt," she said.

For a moment he was absolutely still. Then suddenly he twisted and she found herself swept upward into his arms, his face pressed hard against hers.

"*You're* beautiful," he muttered and his face was drawn with something like pain, something like despair. "Mattie, I've been waiting for you all my life. I don't want to use you as a bandage over my wounds. And I'm scared I will. I'm scared. You deserve so much more than I can give you."

"But you give me so much, Jace," she murmured and held his rigid, resistive body fiercely hard. "You're everything I want. I love you, Jace."

"I . . ."

She could feel the struggle in him. Then the intensity of his mouth on hers said everything he could not bring himself to say.

He could play her like a harp. He enjoyed caressing her, bending her back on sofa or bed, his brows knitted with intent concentration and his eyes smiling, while his hands and his mouth and his expert body slid over every inch of her, taking slow, sensual possession of her with thorough, maddening deliberation, until driven half out of her mind she bit that smiling mouth that tormented her so and the storm swept over them again.

But behind the smile, behind the light easy murmur of love talk and laughter, she saw the tension and the stillness in those eyes watching her, knew there was much of him held back and unsurrendered. He was trying to buy her with pleasure, as a substitute for everything else he could not give, and she had no way of convincing him that this was more than enough for her, that she could wait forever for the other as long as he was in her arms.

She liked to watch him as he slept, brooding over him in fascinated tenderness, watching the dark head on the pillow next to hers. Even in sleep that crease of worry remained between his brows and that faint line of strain around the corners of his lips. Even in sleep the tension never really left him.

He would wake with a start, going from sleep to full consciousness in one jerk, and she would see that sudden flicker of doubt in his eyes before he took in her presence and relaxed. "What are you expecting?" she asked once. "That I'm not going to be there one morning?"

But he didn't smile. "Yes."

"You're the one who'll walk away, Jace. And you'll always be able to walk back."

He touched her face. "Keep telling me that. Maybe one day I'll believe it."

Thursday morning the rain stopped and the sun came out, flooding the beach with brilliant light.

"Damn," said Jace with feeling, watching it from the kitchen doorway.

Mattie laughed, her arms around his waist, her cheek against his chest through the unbuttoned edges of the brown cotton shirt which with the cords had been the only thing he had had to wear these past two days.

"No more privacy," she said.

"No more making love anywhere we feel like it. I think we missed the dining-room table," he said thoughtfully. "Want to try the dining-room table while we still have time?"

"Jace!" She felt him smiling against the top of her head.

Then they both heard the crunch of gravel on the path coming up from the dock.

"Damn it," he said between his teeth. "Why can't we be on a desert island somewhere? We have troubles enough as it is."

He let her go and strode onto the back porch. She followed him.

Len Daviot came around the side of the house, stopped when he saw them.

"Sorry. I was down on the pier, but nobody was there."

"Did you want to take the *Queen* out, Len?" Mattie asked, a little startled to see him. "The weather..."

"No, no." He indicated the business suit he wore. "I'm on my way to the site. I just came to ask a favor of Jace."

"Go ahead," said Jace, surprised.

"Someone told me you're an expert on underwater work, submersibles, suchlike."

Mattie felt Jace tense.

"You could say that."

"I don't know if Mattie told you. My outfit's building this deep-sea lab just off Key Blanca in the middle keys."

Jace nodded. "I heard something about that. A whole undersea city, isn't it? Plus a sea farm all around. Quite an expensive project."

"An experiment in deep-water living. It'll take a couple of years to construct and, once the scientists move in, they'll be using it for the next couple of decades." Len hesitated, enthusiasm checked by Jace's complete lack of interest. "I need your help."

"I'm not a scientist, Len."

"I want your knowledge of deep-water work. My expert on pressure formulas and submersibles is off in Baja somewhere, hasn't turned up when he should have and we can't reach him. I've got a good team. They've put together something they say will work to cover the next couple of days. But Mattie will tell you I like second opinions."

"He had me and Sam check out the seabed for them a year ago," Mattie said quietly.

"And she found a flaw. Second opinions are why there hasn't been an accident on that project since the day it started a year ago," said Len flatly.

"Your team isn't going to appreciate an outsider butting in," Jace said curtly.

Len's face hardened, geniality vanishing into a controlled ruthlessness that showed why he had been chosen to head the project.

"They'll take it and like it. I don't care if it bruises their sensitive egos, I'm not going to risk money and equipment."

"Or lives," Jace murmured.

"Yes," said Len, not listening.

He looked at Jace and Jace looked back, his face that stony, resistive mask.

"A couple of hours of your time," Len said. "That's all it would take."

Jace looked down at the rail he was leaning on, flicked away a few stray grains of sand irritably.

"Len..."

"I wouldn't be asking if it wasn't important," said Len quickly, making it impossible to refuse.

Jace gave him a flat stare of distaste, but Len rode it out admirably. He had developed a skin like a rhinoceros where his project was concerned and was fully prepared to plead, bully and bribe his way to what he wanted. Jace recognized that and the corner of his mouth twisted downward impatiently.

"All right," he said with reluctance.

"Say around one," said Len quickly. "Get it out of your way fast. Mattie can bring you out on the *Queen*. Jace, I really appreciate this."

"Sure," said Jace, looking as if he'd like to recall his words. But Len was already off, moving fast to prevent that happening.

"Jace, what's wrong?" Mattie asked in surprise. His reluctance was unlike him; he was usually the first to help in any circumstance.

He was looking down at his hands clenched on the rail.

"It always comes back, Mattie," he said softly. "The real world. It always comes back."

She didn't know what he meant by that and he didn't elaborate, was silent all the way to Key Blanca.

To her inexperienced eye, the site was a chaos of metal shacks and storage sheds, trailers, heavy equipment, fuel dumps, plastiflex and concrete shells, pipes, cables, components she couldn't even identify.

"Professional," said Jace, his narrow glance swiftly and comprehensively cataloguing the site, obviously seeing something she wasn't. His face was oddly hard and set, a challenging face. He looked as if he were going into a battle instead of simply an informal discussion.

She glanced sideways at him. He had his hands in his pockets, and was walking along with his shoulders hunched.

Len waved to them from the hut nearest the dock, looking incongruous in his neat blue business suit.

Mattie had never been inside the unprepossessing metal hut that the project was using as an office and the interior came as a shock to her. It was like something one might expect to find on the top of some multistory office tower: partitions creating a series of inner rooms, paneled walls, carpeting, high-tech furniture, graphs and computers everywhere. Every detail city-suave, down to the three-piece business suits on most of the men in the boardroom into which they were shown.

Mattie blinked. Jace did not. Mattie saw that he had been expecting something like this.

He shook hands blandly with the men in business suits, ignoring the fact that in his scuffed windbreaker, faded work shirt, cutoffs, and boat shoes, he looked like a tramp.

Mattie realized that the beach-bum appearance was deliberate. She had not thought of it before; on the *Queen*, out there on the site, it had seemed perfectly natural. But he had known what this place would be like. It was a defiance—his clothes, his careless slouching stance.

Mattie came sharply alert.

Not one to miss an opportunity, Len got her to check out charts of the seabed with the construction boss. She did so with only half her attention, watching Jace and the others intently as they bent over the schematics spread across the boardroom table.

She'd had some experience in scuba diving, so was able to follow the conversation in the beginning when they were talking about air mixtures. But then they got into the technicalities of deep-water craft and submersibles, and after that the conversation ran right away from her. She could tell from Len's face that it had run away from him, too; he was an administrator, had no knowledge of the technical aspects of the project he was heading.

Jace was a different matter.

It took no more than a couple of minutes for her to realize that he was in his element. Absorbed in the schematics, he had forgotten his original reluctance. His face was tight with concentration, his eyes narrowed and hard with thought, alive and glittering with the force of his mind behind them as they flashed up to emphasize a point.

He was a different man, the man she had sensed behind the idling motor. Even the set of his body had changed, coming erect, taut as a wound spring as he leaned on one arm over the schematics, effortlessly authoritative. Something about him—manner, stance, gesture—brought the ghost of a blue uniform to hover around him, the memory of gold braid to cling to the flapping sleeve of that arm moving with such surety over the schematics.

The men were listening, nodding even as they argued with him. They were not just business suits, those men; they were professionals. She saw with a shock that he was one of them.

This was where he belonged, some place like this where he could use that wealth of knowledge stored in his brain.

He looked happy. She saw that with an aching pang. He was happy with her. He needed her. But this, too, was necessary to him. It completed him, made him whole.

He knew it. This was what he had been afraid of discovering when he came here, why he had been so reluctant to come.

Watching him, she knew that sooner or later he would have to leave. He was clinging to their sleepy little salvage business, trying desperately to force himself to be content with that. But he would fail. He was not yet ready to admit this to himself, but sooner or later he would have to face it. And then he would leave. He would have to. Without the *Queen* and the charters she would wither and die. So would he, without something like this.

They were both very silent on the boat going home.

Eight

Everyone was back by the time they got there. Gramps had called the boat yards when he'd got no answer at the house and Bob and Sam had picked him up at the airport.

"You got the loan!" Mattie said at once, looking at Bob's jubilant face.

"And the releases," Bob said, grinning from ear to ear. "Now we go get that barge."

"Not so fast, hotshot," growled Gramps. "We can't bring up something that size with just the *Marilee* and the *Queen*. We'll have to finish converting the *Marilee* into a real workboat, lease or buy another to keep her company. We're gonna need them from now on, maybe even a couple more once we really get going."

Bob's eyes glazed over, clearly envisioning an entire fleet.

"Let's get this worked out," Gramps said enthusiastically. "Mattie, where's your calculator? Sam, get Hanlan's price list."

The planning took most of the night. Around eleven, Sam went to bed, but Bob and Gramps were on a roll, too excited to sleep.

Mattie caught Jace's eye over their oblivious heads, laughed involuntarily at the look of frustration on his face.

"I'm off to bed," she said. "I've got that Wanamaker party booked for tomorrow. Good night, everyone."

"Yeah," said Gramps over his shoulder, not listening. "Hey, Jace, how about we do it this way?"

Jace pushed the door to the hall open for her, caught her hand as she went by, pulling her against his side. For a moment they leaned against each other, interlinked fingers tightening.

"This could go on all night," he muttered. "Otherwise I'd ask you to wait for me in the beachhouse."

"And if I didn't have to be up at first light, I'd wait," she murmured.

He turned a little so that his body blocked her from view, kissed her swiftly, his mouth hot and hard. Her fingers clenched in his belt, pulling him to her.

"Damn it," he said against her mouth. "You like playing with fire, don't you? Get out of here."

Mattie laughed and went.

But it was hard to sleep that night without his warmth at her side and his arm heavy upon her waist. The man was addictive; someone should stick a label on him.

She floated through the next day in a daze, her body on automatic pilot while her mind drifted and dreamed. For the first time in her life she was impatient to get home from a charter. The Wanamakers thanked her sincerely for a good day when she dropped them off at their resort and she was both relieved to find that she had functioned so well and a little stunned that she could not remember one single event out of that whole day.

When she brought the *Queen* home, she found both Sam and Jace still hard at work on the *Marilee* even though the sun was almost at the horizon.

Jace looked up and smiled when he saw her, not the wry lift of the right corner of his mouth but that rare genuine smile full of warmth and affection and uncomplicated pleasure that always shook her when she saw it. A little breathless she leaned on the rail of the *Queen*, watching him as he went on working, enjoying the sight of that sure body in motion.

Then she frowned suddenly.

He had set a pace that clearly was the one he had long been accustomed to and right now he seemed comfortable with it. But Mattie could see that if he kept it up it wouldn't be long before his back started hurting.

She grabbed a six-pack from the *Queen*'s cooler, went swiftly up *Marilee*'s gangway.

"Anybody want a beer?"

"Great idea," said Sam promptly. He came and snapped one free, sat down on the deck, his back against the gunwale.

Mattie handed one to Jace as he sat down on a pile of lumber heaped on the deck.

"Boy, you've really made inroads on this," she said, looking around the cluttered deck.

"Yeah, it was a good day's work," said Jace with satisfaction.

"Surely there's no need to push yourselves."

"Oh, we took a break every now and then."

"When we remembered," muttered Sam under his breath, and his and Mattie's eyes met.

Mattie ran her hands lightly over the straight line of Jace's shoulders, enjoying the feel of him. Under her testing fingers, his muscles felt tense but not too strained. His hands came up at once to hers, drew her forward to lean against his back. She looked down worriedly at the top of his head.

"I'm glad it's going so well," she said. "Do you have much more to do or are you ready to quit for the day?"

Jace squinted at the setting sun, then at the cluttered deck. "Why not? There's nothing that can't wait till tomorrow." He stretched. "I'm ready for a shower."

Salt sticky, Mattie nodded. "Me, too."

"Best offer I've had all day."

She pushed at him, laughing. "Get out of here, you!"

He grinned at her and went down the gangway. His walk was springy and his back was moving well.

"Well, it seemed to go all right today," she murmured.

Sam looked up at her. "Yeah, but it'll get worse. He's a stubborn son, that one. He won't make any allowances."

"Sam, couldn't you...?"

"Hell, Mattie, don't you think I been trying? You can't just tell him to knock it off 'cause he'd up and tell you where to put that. I tried speeding up a little so's I could be doing more than he was, but he just speeded up himself, thinking he wasn't pulling his weight, I guess, so I quit. Anyway it would have burned me out for sure; he sets a tough enough pace as is."

"I noticed."

"Yeah. Then I tried slowing down, thinking he'd slow down too, given a chance. But he just started doing things I should've been doing and of course he didn't say anything and, hell, Mattie, I never did like feeling like a slacker. So we're right back at square one."

"Damn."

"It's a great technique if you think about it," Sam said with wry admiration. "He don't argue and he don't get mad, just looks you right in the eye and keeps on doing whatever he wants to do 'cause he thinks it's right. You can't do anything with a man like that."

Mattie sighed. "I know just what you mean, Sam."

The beachhouse was dark when she stepped into it that night, only one light turned on low in the one bedroom. Jace's arms came around her the moment she stepped through the door, his body coming against hers, pushing her back against the door he closed with one thrust of his hand.

"I missed you," he said. "One night and I missed you."

She could not answer because his mouth was on hers, devouring her. They kissed slowly, deeply, mouths twisting. Her hands slid lingeringly over him, drunk on the changing textures of naked back and hips and strong legs. He leaned fully on her, pressing her hard against the door, and she laughed in her throat and bit him softly.

"I feel like a kid again," he said, his breath warm against her face. They stood in a wash of moonlight and shadow, leaning into each other. His gaze moved over her face, smiling, dark with a rueful tenderness. "Waiting for my girl to come through the door, counting the minutes, unable to keep still. Feeling as if the world is new again, as if anything is possible."

She stretched up on tiptoe to wind her arms around his neck, pulling him to her.

"It is."

He made an ambiguous sound in his throat, kissed the fine triangle between her eyes then the tip of her nose. He turned sideways a bit and she made a little protesting murmur before realizing that he was unbuttoning the oversize gauze shirt that was all she was wearing.

"I like the way you come visiting," he said.

She scored his buttocks lightly with her nails. "I like the way you welcome guests."

They laughed softly. He slid the shirt from her shoulders and she pressed closer to him to allow it to fall around her feet.

"Gold and rose and ivory and shadow." His hands moved slowly, lingeringly, over her and she trembled and leaned against him. "You're dream stuff, Mattie; you're something forbidden, something I shouldn't have."

"Listen to me," she murmured. "There's nothing I give you that I don't want to give you. So there's no such thing as something you shouldn't have. Do you understand that?"

"No."

"Okay, let's get down to basics. I can't have you unless you have me. That's the way it works. And I want you."

He started to laugh. "Why does your cockeyed logic always leave me at a loss for words?"

"Because my cockeyed logic is right."

"Sure."

Her knees were weak under the slow knowledgeable knead and rasp of his hands on her body. She let them give, pulling him downward. Then they were both on the floor, tangled together, breathless and laughing, his hand protecting the back of her head.

"There is such a thing as a bed," he murmured.

"But we're never going to make it unless you stay in it."

He moved his open mouth across her face. "That is going to be difficult."

"It might have its compensations."

She felt him smiling as he thought about that. "Are you going to put on the whole show, garter belts and everything?"

She choked with laughter, ran her nails lightly along his flanks in warning. "Are you already at the stage where you need that kind of stimulation, Wyatt?"

His face came lightly against hers. "Oh, babe, I'm in trouble when you just turn your head."

She knew what he meant, had melted inside herself just at the sight of an unexpected angle of his body or the lift of his eyes or that sudden transfiguring smile.

"Promise me something," she said intensely. "Let tomorrow come when it will. Don't question; don't worry. Just live in the present. Can you do that? Just for a little while?"

He kissed her softly. "Make our own personal Eden at the eye of the storm? That I can promise. You make it so easy to do that, Mattie."

She didn't miss the implication that he did not expect it to last. But then neither did she. It was enough just to hold him, enough to lose herself in the golden days, the unbearably sweet nights, to forget tomorrow and live in the ever-present now and see his face relax and the crease between his brows lighten as the days ran on and on.

Work progressed swiftly on *Belle* and the two work-boats, and even with Jace pushing the limits of his endurance every day, nothing had ever gone so well; life had never been so sweet and they all felt it.

"When's this conversion going to be finished?" Bob demanded, but even he was not as impatient as before, steadier now that his dreams were becoming reality.

Jace shifted a little. He had wedged himself unconsciously a little sideways in the corner of the couch where the vee shape would support his back. His fingers sifted absently through Mattie's hair as she sat on the floor, leaning back against his long legs.

"Wednesday," he said.

They both looked at him in surprise and he looked back, smiling a little.

"Next Wednesday," he repeated. "Think you can wait that long, genius?"

"Terrific!" Bob scrabbled through the mess of papers spread out over the coffee table. "Where's that list of supplies I made up?"

Mattie was frowning up at Jace, her head tipped back against his knee. He looked worn and the curves of bone just below his eyes were flattened and sharply visible like those of a tired child's. In weariness he looked very young.

"You shouldn't have set a deadline," she said.

He stroked her face lightly, palm sliding over her cheek, pressing her head to his knee.

"It'll be done by then, Mattie. Don't worry."

"You two can canoodle later; you do it all the time anyway," said Bob impatiently. "Just take a look at this list, Jace, will you? If it's okay, I'll go get that stuff tomorrow."

Jace ran a hand over his face then up over his eyes, looked quizzically from under it at Mattie's hot face.

"I'd like a beer," he said, trying not to laugh.

"I'll get it," she murmured in relief, blushing. "Bob?"

"Huh? Oh, yeah, sure, Mattie."

She had her color under control by the time she came back, but a bubble of irrepressible laughter was stuck in her throat. It faded only when she saw the set of Jace's shoulders as he leaned forward, elbows on his knees, checking Bob's list.

"I haven't got anything to add," he said, handing it back. "Gramps might. Check with him."

"Right."

Mattie handed them their beers, came and sat on the back of the low sofa. Jace's breath left him quickly as her hands closed over the tendons between his neck and shoulders. He leaned back, his eyes closing involuntarily.

"You're pushing that back of yours," she said.

"It's all right," he said flatly.

"The *Belle* can wait awhile," Bob said. His eyes were steady and very level when Jace looked at him in surprise. "I'd rather give you and Sam a hand. After all," he said offhandedly, "the workboats are more important."

The right corner of Jace's mouth tilted in amusement. "All right."

"Go to bed," Mattie said quietly.

"Yes, ma'am," he said obediently, but his eyes were bright with laughter.

When she came into the beachhouse a little while later, he was lying flat on his stomach in bed, reading a book, his chin propped up on a wadded pillow. He turned onto his elbow as she came in, watched her with lazy, intent pleasure as she tugged her T-shirt over her head, stepped out of sandals, cutoffs and underwear.

Then she snatched up his discarded shirt and shrugged into it.

"Hey!" he protested.

"Shut up," she said and came and pushed him flat on his stomach again. He laughed and let her, then gave a little grunt of pleasure and relief as her hands worked down his spine.

"God, Mattie, that feels good," he said on a shudder of breath.

"Jace, don't you ever learn? Why do you keep pushing yourself?"

"Hey, a man's gotta do what a man's gotta do," he murmured, amused.

"Funny man."

He stretched under her hands, luxurious cat stretches, his chin on his crossed wrists upon the wadded pillow. His eyes were closed with pleasure, his mouth smiling. She saw that this was all the answer she was going to get. He showed his pleasure, but he never shared his pain, bottled it up behind wisecracks and that determined silence.

When he was again relaxed and content under her hands, she sat back on her heels. He turned his head, looked up at her, smiling.

"Now come down here and let me do that to you."

She reached out abruptly and rolled him over onto his back. It took all her strength. He looked up at her, wide-eyed with surprise, half laughing.

"What's the matter?"

"Stop shutting me out, Jace," she said quietly.

She saw the shock in his face.

"Mattie, I'm not!"

"Yes, you are. You do it all the time."

She could see the thoughts flying behind his still eyes, that quick intelligence rapidly shifting through everything that might cause her to say something like that.

Then he sat up and took her face very gently in his hands.

"Maybe I do," he said. "I don't mean to. It's a reflex with me."

"I know that. Why is it?"

"I . . ." He drew a long breath and she felt him struggling against the barriers of his own reticence. "Mattie, look, I learned a long time ago that people don't want to be bothered with someone else's pain."

She stared at him.

"That's the most dismal thing I've ever heard," she said sharply. "Jace, maybe that's good enough for acquaintances, but it's not good enough for the people who care for you!"

He looked at her in silence and his eyes did not waver. She caught her breath. Even from people who are supposed to care for you, that steady gaze was saying.

"So you keep it to yourself, deal with it yourself, come back only when it's all settled, is that it?"

"That's it," he said flatly.

"No!" she said furiously. "I don't know about all those other people you seem to have met, but I don't operate that way! If you're happy, I want to share it. If you're hurting, I want to help!"

"What if there's nothing you can do?" he challenged. "Should I still burden you with it? You asked me why I keep pushing myself. All right, I'll tell you. Because what I can do with my hands is the last thing left me out of all the things I'm capable of doing and I'm damned if I'm going to give that up too. Now," he said, "can you change that, Mattie?"

"Sharing things can help, Jace," she said quietly. "Talking about them can help. One day you'll see that."

"Maybe," he muttered, unconvinced.

"Someday when you've learned to trust again."

His hands tightened around her face. "I do trust you, Mattie."

She drew his face to hers, kissed him very gently.

"No, not yet. But one of these days, Jace. One of these days, maybe."

She was prepared to wait. But there were too many things unresolved between them, too much held back and unsurrendered. And time was short.

It didn't help that Len Daviot kept coming around. Just to talk, he said, but he always brought his briefcase with him when he came and there were always papers from it clutched in his fist when he left.

Jace was not the only one who got tense when Len came. Mattie hated his coming. It was a reminder of the life Jace should be leading, and she kept waiting for Jace to realize that.

After a few visits, Jace started looking merely amused, but Mattie never stopped hating it.

"What does he want all the time?" she asked once as Len was leaving.

Jace was sitting on the porch rail where Len had left him. He looked after Len, his face half amused, half exasperated. Mattie came and leaned on his shoulder to remind him she was there.

"Decisions," Jace said.

"What?"

"He wants me to make technical decisions for him." He looked around at her, amused. "He's got a good team, but he can't seem to trust them. Oh, it's not all his fault. They seem to do things by committee up there, every man putting in his nickel's worth. There's no one to pull all the strings together except Len. They bring him about five or six different ways to handle a problem and being an administrator not a technican he can't tell which one is right."

"I don't understand. All that high-powered staff and they keep coming up with mistakes?"

"No, no, Mattie. They come up with several different perfectly correct solutions. Every one of them right as rain. Do you know what I do? I just point at one at random and say: that one."

Mattie started to laugh. "You're kidding."

He too was laughing. "Seriously. Confidence seems to be the only problem. They don't have confidence in him because he doesn't have the necessary technical knowledge, and he doesn't have confidence in them for the same reason."

"Why doesn't he get an assistant?"

"He doesn't want to share the power," he said simply and she drew back and stared at him in surprise.

But he was right. There was that about Len, under the geniality and the camaraderie, that liking for power, that jealousy about it.

She stroked his flat cheek lightly, turning his face to hers. "Does it bother you, his coming around?"

He drew a harsh breath. "I don't want to remember," he admitted.

He couldn't shut it out forever. Sooner or later he would have to face it. But she could not say that. She was clinging to every day, every moment. She never touched him without thinking that this touch might be the last, and that awareness made each touch, the smallest caress, infinitely precious, poignantly sweet, never to be taken for granted.

"What are you thinking?" he asked, but she shook her head, kissed him softly and smiled when his arms tightened around her waist.

Sam called him from the deck of the workboat just as he pulled her to him.

"Damn." He kissed her between her breasts, pressing his face hard against her. "Save my place."

She laughed and he grinned at her over his shoulder as he went down the steps. She leaned on the rail, watching him, holding on to the moment.

Nine

Wednesday the workboats were ready and they started to load Bob's chemicals and equipment.

Delkote sent around lagniappe from his bar, underwater shots of the barge that he had acquired from a diver he knew. They were delighted, pored over them, scrutinizing the sunken barge and the seabed on which she lay.

"These are great!" Bob exclaimed, grinning from ear to ear. "God bless Del! We can see exactly how she's lying!"

"What I can see is that she's balanced right on the edge of a fissure," said Sam, tracing the line of it with his forefinger. "There. No telling how deep that is. We start tearing out bulkheads, shifting her weight, we might rock her, tip her right over into it. Another thing, that fissure's on the edge of Len Daviot's territory."

"That won't matter," Bob said. "We won't be interfering with their operation at all. We're nowhere near where they're working and it's open sea, anyway. She slips, we just go after her wherever she settles."

"Depends on how deep it is." Jace glanced up at Sam. "You and I'll check that out first thing, okay?"

"Might be real deep, Jace," Sam muttered.

"Got a problem with that, Sam?"

"Maybe Bob and I should check it out. Not you."

Jace jerked his head up to stare at him. "Why the hell not me? I've racked up more time in a wet suit than the whole bunch of you put together."

"That was a lot of hash marks ago."

"Thanks a lot."

"Jace..." That was Gramps, looking embarrassed. "It's not the experience. Hell, we know you got the experience. It's your back."

He straightened, shocked and angry. He had not expected to fight this battle all over again, bitterly resented it being revived at this time and place.

Gramps's gaze fell before his. He looked around at the others. Bob was avoiding his eyes, his gaze embarrassedly fixed on the shots. Sam was watching him, his round face determined. Mattie, perched on one of the drums of Bob's chemicals, was hugging her upraised knee and frowning. Her clear, level eyes were steady on his and shadowed with worry.

They were united against him in this. He could see that it was misplaced concern for him that moved them, but that only made it more bitter. They could not see that it was more important to him to dive, that their concern could cripple him more than the piece of iron in his back.

"Look, Jace," said Gramps, spokesman for them all. "The navy said a certain kind of pressure, certain kind of exertion could cause that splinter to shift. You go down there, you start working at those depths, you'll kill yourself sure. We can't let you risk something like that through pure boneheadedness."

"It's my back, Gramps, and I know how much it will take."

"No, you don't, son. There's nobody knows that. And you could put yourself in a pine box finding it out. Know your limits? Hell, you keep pushing your limits. All of us know that. One of these days you're gonna push them too far. Topside's one story; down there's another. Can't let you, son. Just can't."

"I'm going down, Gramps," he said flatly. He was angry at all of them for not understanding. He felt almost betrayed. It was so clear to him why he could not let himself be defeated by something like this that he could not see why they could not understand something so simple.

Gramps threw up his arms in exasperation. "Mattie, sometimes you talk his language better'n anyone. You tell him."

Jace looked at Mattie. She was very pale and the clear blue of her eyes was dark with anxiety as she looked back at him.

It was a choice she should not have been forced to make—a choice between his safety and his confidence in himself. It was asking too much of her to understand, so he did not ask it, stood looking at her gravely, demanding nothing of her.

But behind his control he felt that old uncontrollable surge of bitterness and betrayal, suddenly felt very alone.

He saw her hands clench, her head lift to speak, braced himself because he would have to refuse her just as he had refused the others. And he knew that would hurt her, and he knew things would never be the same again between them.

"You do what you have to, Jace," she said very steadily. "They're wrong."

Everyone gaped at her and she looked back, her gaze level.

"You have to stop treating people like children, Gramps," she said. "It's his back and his life and he's got his reasons. Leave him alone."

Jace felt as if something had hit him hard right in the solar plexus, driving out all his breath.

She had listened to him; she had really heard him. She had understood.

Sharing can help, she had suggested before, even if it didn't change things. He had not heard her. Now he understood. Nothing had changed—and yet everything had changed. He did not feel alone. And that was a wonderful feeling—that hand stretched out to him in both trust and support, that love that did not operate solely on the surface of things.

"Mattie," he said, then stopped. There was too much he wanted to say and this was neither the time nor the place for it. After a moment he said the only words that summed up what he was feeling. "Thank you."

She nodded, but her gaze was anxious.

"I will be careful," he said and now she smiled, knowing that he meant it.

"All right then," said Sam, looking at Mattie, and Gramps threw up his hands in disgust.

"You're all nuts!" He stamped over to the *Marilee*. "Can we get this tub loaded? You can stare at them fool pictures when the work's done."

Sam grinned. "Gramps always did hate losing an argument. We'd better get moving or he'll be on the jump all day. I'll get the hoist."

Bob and Jace finished loading the sling, then Jace rode the load up onto the *Marilee*'s deck where he and Sam unloaded it. They had it down to a science by now, worked fast and smoothly, Bob and Mattie loading the sling, Sam and Jace unloading it and stowing or lashing down its contents while Gramps supervised, yelling when anything was not to his liking.

In a few hours they had it done.

"Last one," called Mattie and hopped on top of the load as Bob finished hooking the sling and waved to send it away.

Sam punched the button that started the hoist.

The load inched up smoothly. Then at its apex, the sling slipped.

Bob yelled and threw himself backward as a crate fell, brushing his shoulder before it slammed into the ground.

Jace flung himself sideways over crates to grab the rope.

"Sam! Get over here, Sam!"

The sling slipped even more, drums spilling and thudding to the ground, crates smashing open on the concrete. Mattie was scrambling over the drums rolling under her feet, holding grimly on to the netting of the sling.

It had happened just this way the last time, Jace thought in a vivid unwanted flash of memory; not in the events of it, but in the terrible speed and the confusion and the panic. Everything coming apart the way it always did when things went wrong, with disastrous speed and thoroughness. That time it had ended in death and pain: that crash of the explosion, white water turning red under the blinding lights, Frank DiMarco dead, that shock wave smashing him forward to drown in white light and pain.

Not this time. Not this time.

He threw his weight on the rope just as the hook of the sling snapped.

Mattie cried out involuntarily as the hook tore down her leg in its backlash.

Then all the weight of the several hundred pounds that had been on the metal cable slammed onto the rope.

That's it, he thought as his back wrenched. Terror for her had driven caution from his mind. The flaming stab of agony that shot through his spine took away sight and sound and hearing. But if he could just hold on to the rope, it would be worth it.

Then air tore into his lungs and he could breathe again. Sam was beside him, grabbing at the rope he had not let go, and the drums were tumbling free as the sling collapsed, and Mattie was the only weight on the line, still clinging desperately to the swinging net.

He was still there, he realized in astonishment, unable to believe it. Still functioning, and now the pain was receding and his sight beginning to clear. They had all been wrong—the doctors, the navy, everyone. His back could take a lot more than anyone had thought. He was not balanced on a knife-edge, waiting for the ax to fall.

"Damn," he said, almost light-headed with shock and relief. Then coming back to the realization that the thing was not over yet though the major part of the danger was gone, "Mattie, hold on! Oh, babe, hold on!"

She nodded, teeth clenched with effort, clinging grimly to the net. The cut on her leg was bleeding.

He and Sam lowered her as fast as they could without jarring her and causing her to lose her grip. When she came within reach, Bob caught her, taking her weight, then cradled her the rest of the way down.

Jace was down the *Marilee*'s gangway in seconds and on his knees beside her, catching her up as she reached for him, holding her fiercely close.

"Honey, are you all right? Babe! Are you...?"

"I'm all right, I'm fine...." But she was shaking, clinging to him hard, still feeling herself suspended over thin air. "I cut my leg."

Bob was already slitting the seam of her jeans, folding the edges back to check her calf, his hands surprisingly gentle.

"How is it?" Jace demanded.

Bob was smiling. "It'll need a few stitches, but it's not too bad."

"Just a scratch," said Mattie shakily.

"What's with this bite-the-bullet stuff, for God's sake?" he demanded ridiculously. "Damn it, does it hurt?"

"Well, of course it hurts, you idiot," she said and leaned against him and laughed helplessly. "Look who's talking."

He kissed her bruisingly hard, then rose and scooped her up into his arms.

"We'd better get you to a doctor."

"I'll get the car," said Bob and ran for it.

"Oh, Jace, your back," Mattie said immediately as he began to carry her up the path. "You shouldn't. I'm too heavy."

"You're no weight," he said and grinned, feeling the dull throb that had settled into his lower back, a throb like a toothache, nothing he could not handle. "My back's great. The navy, the hospital, all those doctors, they were all wrong. Mattie, I wrenched it. I really wrenched it. And nothing happened. I'm still here."

Her arms tightened around his neck. "Jace..."

"Oh, it aches," he admitted. "Like a bad tooth. But, Mattie, it can take a lot more than anybody thought it would. I just have to be a little careful, that's all."

"Oh, Jace," she said and hugged him tightly. Suddenly the world was a very nice place to be.

Bob had the car in front of the path. Sam had sensibly run for the first-aid box. He brought it out to the car and they got a temporary bandage on her leg, settled her in the back with her left leg stretched out along the seat.

"I'll take her," Jace said flatly and the others nodded, acknowledging his right.

"We'll finish loading," Sam said. "You take care of her, hear?"

"I hear." Jace smiled reassuringly at Gramps who had been standing on the outskirts all this time, unusually silent and looking very old. "She'll be fine, Gramps."

Gramps jerked his chin in acknowledgment without saying a word.

It was dark by the time they got back from the hospital, Mattie wearing a neat bandage around her calf and walking with only a trace of a limp.

"I feel like a fraud," she said as they fussed over her. "It's just a scratch."

"It always is," murmured Jace and she laughed up at him.

"Where's Gramps?" she asked, looking around. He was conspicuous in his absence.

"I saw him going into the beachhouse," Sam called from the kitchen. "I can hold dinner for half an hour if you two want a chance to take a quick shower."

"Oh, yes, please," said Mattie gratefully. "I smell like the hospital."

"Don't get that bandage wet." Jace was frowning a little. "I'll go see what's bothering Gramps."

All Gramps's actions since the accident had been peculiar. Normally he would have kicked up a fuss of epic proportions when Mattie was hurt. Certainly he should have been front and center when she came home from the hospital.

The lights of the beachhouse were on. Gramps was standing in the middle of the living room, his hands in the pockets of his frayed cutoffs and his gaze on the floor. He spun when Jace came in, stared at him as if he had never seen him before.

"Gramps? Something wrong?"

"Tell me it's not true, what I been thinking," Gramps said and Jace blinked.

"What...?"

"You tell me and I'll believe you, boy. So tell me!"

"Gramps, what's the matter with you?"

Gramps swung violently toward him, then stopped himself with an effort, gripping his hands tightly together.

"Don't play dumb. Maybe I been a sucker; maybe I been dumb—and deaf and blind. But not no more, boy. I got my eyes opened by you today on that pier."

"Gramps," said Jace patiently. "I don't know what you're talking about."

"Mattie, that's what I'm talking about!" Gramps exploded. "What the hell else?"

Jace sat down abruptly on the arm of the battered couch.

They had never thought how it might look, their keeping it from the others. It had just happened, without a word being spoken between them, half from a desire for privacy, half from a dislike of the possibility of having their relationship discussed while it was still in that fragile state of exploration and ambiguity. Neither of them had ever thought that their reserve might be taken as guilt.

"So it's true," said Gramps as the silence lengthened.

"Yes."

"Why'd you do it? Tell me that. Why?"

Jace was silent.

"I trusted you, Jace. There's no one in the world I would have trusted more'n you."

"Gramps, listen, we..."

"No! No 'we'; there's no 'we' about it! You!"

Jace's head came up sharply.

"We," he repeated flatly. "Do you think I forced her? We wanted each other. That's natural and we're not ashamed of it. Mattie and I..."

"No!" Gramps whirled on him. "I don't want to know! I don't want to know what the two of you have done! I don't want to think about it!"

Jace rose slowly to his feet as if pulled by strings like a puppet.

"It's obscene," whispered Gramps and Jace looked at him in shock.

"Gramps," Jace said carefully, "that's a hell of a loaded word."

"It's the right word. I know all them fancy words and that's the right one. For God's sake, Jace, she's a child!"

"She's an adult," said Jace tightly. "She's not your 'golden child,' Gramps. She's of age, with all the privileges that entails, and she's entitled to make her own decisions."

"The hell!"

They faced each other in dangerous silence.

"You pack your things and you get out of here," Gramps said through clenched teeth. "You be off my property come morning. You been my friend for fourteen years, otherwise I'd beat you silly."

There was a small sharp silence. Then:

"All right," said Jace.

"I don't want to look at you again. I don't want to think about you. You were like a son to me, Jace. Boy, I loved you. But you ain't no friend of mine no more."

"All right, Gramps," Jace repeated very quietly. "I'll pack and I'll leave, but you're going to listen to me first."

"Ain't nothing you can say could excuse this."

"No excuses," Jace said flatly. "No blame; no excuses. But you're going to hear me out."

"I'll send your money after you, every red cent of it," Gramps said, not listening. "You leave me an address."

"Sit down, Gramps. We're going to talk about Mattie."

"Mattie's not your concern!"

"No, she's her own. But you're screwing up her life and I'm not going to let you do that any longer."

"Me!" Gramps yelled.

Jace gave him a flat, hard stare.

"Where do you get off telling me *I*..."

"Sit down, Gramps!"

The sudden blaze of anger set Gramps right back on his heels. He sat down suddenly.

"A child," said Jace tightly. "What's the voting age, Gramps? What's the age of consent? What's the legal age of maturity?"

"It's got nothing to do with legal age!"

"She's twenty-four, Gramps! When are you going to see her as what she is? How old does she have to be to fall in love, get married, have kids? Thirty? Forty? When? Or are you going to keep this up forever?"

Gramps coughed, too angry for breath, too confused for answers.

"You're hurting her, Gramps. Can't you see that? You're suffocating her and finally she'll have enough of it and she'll have to break away just to breathe. And even that will hurt her because she loves you and she loves this place."

"How do I...?" wheezed Gramps. "When did I ever...?"

"I've been talking to Sam. You're right. It's got nothing to do with legal age. How long has she been running this business of yours? Sawyer Salvage and Charter. It should have read Thornton, because she's been running it since she was sixteen. She's been making all the decisions, taking care of all the problems and even Sam's been only an arm to carry out her orders. Did you even ask her before you sold half the business to me, Gramps?"

Gramps reared back defensively. "Sure I did! But then she started this business with the *Queen* and..." His voice petered out in sudden realization.

"She had to, didn't she, to get something of her own? All the charters ask for her; every charter-boat skipper from Key Largo to Key West trusts her to know what she's doing. But not you. For you she's still ten years old and you're going to keep her that way."

Gramps shook his head dully.

"You have to stop, Gramps. She's bright and she's beautiful and she's too good to waste."

There was a long silence.

"You hear me, Gramps?"

Gramps sighed deeply. "I hear you."

"Do you understand?"

"Hell, I'm not senile. I understand. I just didn't want to let her go, I guess." He sighed again. "You're right and I'm wrong. I guess I been wrong about a lot of things."

"Yeah."

"I'm sorry. Okay? I'm sorry. What do you want? My blessing? Okay, you got my blessing. You love her? You want to marry her? Okay, I won't kick up a..."

He stopped at the sudden flicker of movement in Jace's face.

There was a sharp silence.

Then Gramps said in a whisper, "You do want to marry her, don't you, boy?"

Jace said nothing at all.

"What was all that about then?" Gramps demanded, his voice rising. "Hell, you're telling me she's got a right to get married and have kids and all that, and I think you got a stake in that somewheres. But now you're telling me I was right all along? You're telling me all you wanted was a good time?"

Jace was looking down at his hands and his face was harsh and more resistive than Gramps had ever seen it.

"I'll leave tonight, Gramps," he said in a flat, final voice.

Gramps stared at him, and he looked up and his eyes were a stranger's eyes, cold and hard and uncaring.

"I don't understand," Gramps mumbled. "I just don't understand anything at all."

Jace got up and began moving around the room, collecting things. He didn't say a word and he acted as if Gramps were not in the room at all. After a while, Gramps got to his feet and went away, moving very slowly and heavily.

Bob and Sam were setting the table in the dining room and Mattie was in the kitchen, pouring herself a glass of water, when Gramps came in the door. She looked up, smiling.

"What kept you? Dinner's ready."

Gramps leaned on the counter, avoiding her gaze.

"How's your leg?" he muttered.

"Fine." She flipped the long skirt of her blue silk robe back to show him, then frowned as he nodded dully. "What's wrong, Gramps?"

"Mattie..." he said wretchedly and at his tone her eyes widened. Her gaze shot past him, searching.

"Where's Jace?"

"I—I said . . . I got things all wrong and I said . . ."

Mattie grabbed his shoulders. "Gramps, what did you do?"

"He's packing to leave and I don't know how to stop him."

Mattie picked up her skirts and ran.

The front door of the beachhouse was open. She landed with a thump against the doorjamb, leaned there panting. Jace glanced at her from where he was standing at the little dining table, methodically packing things into his seabag. His eyes were hooded and his lips were pulled into that tight downward-curving line of strain.

"What did he say to you?" she demanded.

"Nothing that wasn't true." He moved swiftly toward her. "You shouldn't be standing."

The cut on her leg was the last thing on her mind.

"I don't care about that," she said distractedly.

"I care."

He took her gently by the elbows and pressed her into a chair beside the dining table, moved away the moment she was seated. Only his hands had touched her and very lightly, very carefully. But she could feel a vibrating tension in him, a violence rigidly controlled.

She looked at the things on the table, kept her voice steady only by an effort.

"You're leaving."

"Yes."

"Why?"

He came and squatted down on his heels in front of her, his head down, fingers absently brushing away a few stray grains of sand from the strap of her sandal.

"Jace," she insisted.

He looked up at her, his eyelids strained as if he were looking into a glaring light.

"He said I took advantage of you."

"That's not true!"

"It's true. I bawled him out. He was acting as if you were ten years old, the way he always does, and somehow I lost my temper." He smiled crookedly. "I only just figured out why. Because it was easier to get mad at him, easier to put the blame on him instead of where it really belonged—on myself. That way I didn't have to face the fact that he was right."

"He was wrong!" she exclaimed, appalled.

He looked down at his hands, then up at her. His face was very still and very vulnerable.

"There I was cussing him out, Mattie, and he's nodding and agreeing, and I'm feeling proud of myself because I'd finally made him understand you have a right to a life of your own. And then he said: You love her. You want to marry her. I won't kick up a fuss. He thought that was what it was all about. And, damn it, that's what it should have been about!" His mouth twisted painfully. "Mattie, I couldn't say yes and I couldn't say no. I *couldn't*."

She put her hand very carefully on his cheek. Her fingers were trembling.

"Jace, I told you. No strings."

"But there should be strings, Mattie!" he said violently and jerked to his feet and strode across the room. "I should never have let you agree to that. I've been exploiting you, Mattie. I finally faced up to that."

"You can't exploit someone who wants to be exploited!"

He laughed with a kind of angry amusement. "Your cockeyed logic! Yes, one can, Mattie. And it's not right."

She stood up, ignoring his movement of protest.

"Everything I've given you I've wanted to give. You haven't been taking advantage of me, Jace. We've only given to each other."

"*You've* given, Mattie. I've been holding out. You know that."

"It doesn't matter."

"It matters. Pleasure for pleasure, that's an even trade. Warm body against body in the cold loneliness of the night, that's even. But you give a lot more, Mattie, and oh, God, I've needed it. But I can't give back. I've got nothing to give you back, and that's wrong. I've been cheating you and I can't do that any longer."

"Jace," she whispered, "you give me so much!"

He moved swiftly toward her, then stopped abruptly even as she caught her breath in hope.

"All my life I've paid my own way," he said in that tight, gritty voice. "This time I didn't have the price. But I wanted it, so I took it, anyway. What does that make me?"

She had been prepared for everything but this. This was crazy, so unlooked for that she had no words, could muster no defence.

"I can't find a way around it," he said. "I've been thinking and thinking. I can't see any other way that's right for either of us."

"You keep thinking I want or need something more than we have," she cried. "I don't. You can take that out of your calculations. If I never had more than this, I'd be content."

"If I'd never come here, you'd have been better off," he retorted.

She was struck absolutely dumb.

"You'd have had a chance to have all the things I can't give you, all the things I want you to have. If I leave, you'd have that chance again."

She wanted to fly at him; she wanted to shake him for his blind obstinacy, his stubborn refusal to listen. What can you do with a man who won't argue and won't get mad, a man who just looks you in the eye and keeps right on doing what he thinks is right? She felt exactly the way Sam had felt, baffled and frustrated and utterly at a loss for words.

"You keep talking about things that don't matter to me," she said angrily. "A chance I don't want; a price I never demanded. Maybe we're talking about the wrong person. Is there a price on you, Jace? Is that why you're leaving—because I didn't pay it?''

He came closer suddenly and caught her shoulders and kissed her hard.

"Do you think I want to leave?" he asked with a harsh breath. "Do you think it's easy for me? You're part of me, Mattie. I'm bleeding trying to break away."

Her whole body cleaved to him, rising like a flame to the despairing intensity of his mouth.

"Then stay," she said fiercely.

He made a sound in his throat like a sound of pain. His hands dragged over the contours of her face, rough and hurtful as never before under the lash of his anger and his desperation. She could see the struggle in his dark, glittering eyes, feel it in the rigidity of that body pressing involuntarily against hers.

He swung her suddenly around so that she was leaning against the table and he was leaning against her, his body urgent, his weight demanding on her. Her head fell back, heavy with heat and surrender; her arms clung desperately around his neck.

But his hands were clenched on the table's edge to keep from gripping her and his body was resistant even as it strained itself to hers.

"I have to think," he said violently between his teeth.

"Don't think," she whispered fiercely. "Just feel. Feel, Jace! What's more true than feeling? Don't you want what we have?"

She felt him shudder and rub involuntarily against her.

"I want it," he muttered. "I'd have sold my soul for it. I did. But I won't sell yours."

"Why not?" she whispered. "It's yours to sell."

His mouth took hers hard, that rigid control of his finally shattered. His hands ripped open her robe, raked

down her flesh with merciless ferocity, uncaring that he
might hurt her, gentleness lost in despairing, uncontrollable need.

But her hands were tearing open his shirt, her body
was straining demandingly to his. He bent her back, his
mouth avid on her breasts, and she cried out with sav-
age satisfaction, dragging him urgently closer.

His arms tore her off the ground. She wound herself
around him. She knew his body better than she did her
own, used her knowledge shamelessly, lost to everything but the feel of him, that maddening pounding of
heat and naked desire between them.

She felt the sensation of motion without truly being
aware of it, realized that he was sweeping her into the
bedroom only when she saw the lintel of the door swim
by over her dazed eyes.

He threw her onto the bed and she reared up to meet
him even as he fell on her.

Anger and despair left no room for gentleness. His
hands bruised, her nails scored his flesh; but no touch
was felt as anything but the most terrible stimulus. The
line between pleasure and pain had blurred long ago and
she cried out in wild abandonment as she felt the edge of
his teeth rake her flesh, his hands rasp intimate and insistent across her body, taking possession of her with
ruthless exacting thoroughness.

She was beyond that now, on fire for him, and her
body moved feverishly, writhing to his, savagely delighted by the violent intensity of his arousal, urging him
on, her hands demanding, dragging at him even as he
twisted her up to meet him, his body probing hers.

He drove forward, taking her with violent, uncontrollable force, and she moaned in unbearable pleasure
as he filled her. She met each lunge of his body with

equal ferocity, keening in his ear, inciting him with voice and hands and mouth and body, reality lost, reason lost in this frenzied, jarring, bone-rattling rhythm that was shockingly fulfilling.

And when that moment of mindless release came, she could have died from the unbearable rapture of it.

He lay spent upon her, shuddering.

"Mattie," he groaned against her temple. "I can't let this go...."

But she heard in his voice that note of despairing finality that told her he would. And she held him tightly, her face buried in his neck, memorizing the feel of him, the scent of him, trying to make the moment last forever.

Her hands were clenched across his back. He pulled them away, forced them against the pillow on either side of her head. His face pressed hard against hers, his body strained for a moment against her, then disengaged itself, began to draw away.

"Oh, Jace, don't," she gasped and his breath shook against her face as he lifted his head.

"It's no good," he said. "No good. Feeling's no solution. For either of us."

"What is, Jace?" she whispered despairingly.

He lay for a moment heavy and lax upon her. Then his eyes closed, his lips tightened.

"I have to think," he said and rolled away.

She sat up as he rose, drawing the coverlet around her, huddling into it, shivering.

He went and got his seabag and brought it back into the bedroom. She watched him dress, his face withdrawn and brooding, his movements swift and certain now that he had made up his mind.

She looked around, for the first time really seeing the room. It had been divested of every trace of his presence—closets, shelves, dresser drawers, the medicine cabinet in the bathroom, all stripped.

"You haven't collected much, have you?" she remarked. The bag was only slightly more bulky than it had been the day he came. Consciously or unconsciously, he had thought of his stay as only temporary.

"Yes," he said, answering her thought rather than her words, the way they always could with each other. "That's exactly right, Mattie."

He hefted the bag, looked around the room. Then he looked at her.

They had grown into each other, atom into atom. In the crucible of the past few months this metal and that metal had fused into this alloy, and they were locked into each other as immutably as iron and carbon into steel.

"When you've finished thinking..."

"Don't wait for me, Mattie," he said flatly.

She looked at him defiantly, her lips trembling into a shaky smile.

"I will if I want to, Jace Wyatt."

"Don't," he said and came and kissed her painfully hard.

Then he pried her hands from their grip on his shirt and picked up his seabag and walked out the door.

Ten

So that was it.

For weeks she kept thinking about what she could have said or done to keep him. But nothing would have made any difference to that struggle that had been going on inside his head from the very beginning.

She went through little flurries of anger and hurt and resentment. None of it helped or made any difference to the way she felt about him. Pride helped, kept her head up in the daytime. But pride was a cold thing to hold on to in the lonely nights.

Len Daviot complained for days when he learned Jace had gone.

"What am I going to do with these proposals?" he kept asking.

"Pick one," said Mattie in exasperation. "That's what he said he did—picked one at random."

But Len didn't believe her.

Then after a couple of weeks he suddenly stopped coming around at all, even to charter a boat.

Mattie ran into him in town and out of curiosity asked him about it in a roundabout fashion by making a joke about his working too hard even to take a day off sailing.

"I can handle the work fine!" he exploded and she stared at him in astonishment. "The day I can't handle anything that's thrown at me's the day hell freezes over!"

"Len, I was just kidding," she said in amazement.

"Sure you were," he retorted and stormed off, leaving her staring.

"It's as if he were feeling guilty about something," Mattie said when she told the others about it that evening. "Does that make sense?"

Bob shrugged. "He's been acting real jumpy lately. I was talking to some of the guys from the site and they say he's been cussing everyone out the past couple of weeks for no reason at all."

"So he's on the prod," Gramps growled, irritated. "So what? We're all jumpy. Things haven't been normal around her since Ja—"

He stopped abruptly.

Everyone pretended to be very busy with what they were doing.

There wasn't such a real difference to their lives, Mattie thought. They had hired a couple of men to run the other workboat; Bob and Sam were handling the salvage beautifully; everything was the same as it had been before Jace came. But somehow the talk in the evenings was hollow. Their family of four had expanded to five, and since he'd left there was a ghost in the living room in the evenings, and a hole in their lives.

Raising the barge was taking a lot longer than they had anticipated. As they had feared, they had dislodged her while working and she had tipped over into the fissure. She settled well and they were still able to reach her, but now bringing her up required suits to work in and a platform to be built as a base of operations. It meant a lot more time and trouble.

Their activity on the boundary of what Len thought of as his territory soon attracted his attention. He shot right over to order them off.

There was no reason why their operation could not work comfortably in the same area of water as his. The barge was nowhere near the lab and neither of them was interfering in any way with the other. But Len's innate caution was exacerbated by whatever was bothering him. When they refused to stop, he hit the roof.

Before they knew it, he was trying to get an injunction against them.

Bob managed to delay that. Legalities took time and while Len complained and wrote furious memos to his superiors in an effort to get their powerful legal machinery in motion, Sawyer Salvage worked as fast as it could to get the barge up before that happened.

"Two months since we started work on that barge," Bob sighed, sprawled on the front stoop at the end of a long day. "I'm exhausted. But we'll be over the hump soon. If Len holds off, we can start pumping the chemicals down into her next week. Hey, Gramps, want to break out the booze and celebrate?"

"Yeah, sure; anything you say, Bob."

But no one moved. Bob looked at them wryly.

"This place is like a morgue," he said.

"Shut up," growled Sam and cast a quick look to see whether Mattie was still busy on the *Queen*. She was and he relaxed.

"Two months," Gramps muttered. "You'd think he'd have written. At least to give us his address. Hell, his money's sitting there in the bank, waiting for him. Both his investment and the profit from the *Belle*. I told him I'd send it after him."

"He never cared for the money, Gramps," said Sam. "He came in because he knew you needed it and because it gave him a place to stay. Guess he figures you still need it."

"Yeah, well, forget the money. I figured he cared about us," muttered Gramps.

Sam started to say something sharp and angry, then stopped.

"All right!" flared Gramps. "I know it was my fault! You don't have to say it."

"It wasn't anybody's fault," said Bob and they looked at him in surprise. "Nothing you could have said would have made any impression on him if that wasn't the way he was thinking already. Why do you think Mattie's never been mad at you, Gramps? She knows."

"I miss him," muttered Gramps. "I really miss him."

Bob patted his shoulder. "We all do, Gramps."

Oddly he was now the steadiest one among them. It was as if with the actualization of his dreams, Bob had found himself. A while ago the setbacks they had with the barge would have driven him right up the wall. Now he dealt with each problem coolly and methodically as it arose, letting nothing keep him from his steady progress toward his goal.

They all looked up as Len screeched his Caddy to a stop in front of the house.

Bob went down the steps to meet him, grinning a little. "Something's wrong, Len?"

"Okay, so you're pals with the sheriff," Len said through his teeth. "But I'll get your rig out of there if I have to have my own men do it."

"Keep it legal, Len," said Bob, amused. "You set foot on that platform without the law behind you, we'll have you up on charges. What's the matter with you anyway? We'll be out of there in a couple of weeks and no harm done."

But Len was in no mood for reason. His geniality had faded the moment they'd crossed swords with him and he was proving a surprisingly obdurate enemy.

"It won't help you going over my head," he said and their jaws dropped. He stood glaring at them, his head down and his feet spread, looking like a bull harassed beyond patience and endurance. "They know my work up there; they know this project's been accident free from the minute it started. I've got friends up there. I told your good buddy last month what I thought about his proposal. It's not going to help him or you to go over my head to the board."

Sam and Gramps were both on their feet.

Len slammed back into his Caddy.

"Len, wait!" exclaimed Bob, but Len was not listening. He shot off as Bob reached for the car door, scattering gravel over Bob's feet.

"Jace? Was that Jace he was talking about?" Gramps looked poleaxed.

They stared at each other.

"Sure sounds like it," Bob said.

"You mean he was here and he didn't come and see us?" Gramps spluttered. "Didn't even call? Didn't bother to remember we was alive?"

"Maybe he had his reasons," said Mattie quietly behind them.

They looked around in surprise, then avoided her eyes.

"No use speculating," said Bob and came and hooked an arm negligently around Mattie's neck. "You through for the day?"

She leaned against him gratefully, trying not to show that she was hurting. "Yes."

"Let's catch a movie. I'm going stir-crazy sitting around here."

"Okay."

Bob was very quiet all through the movie. Glancing at his abstracted face as the credits rolled by, Mattie wondered whether he had seen even one frame of it. She certainly had not, so that made two of them.

"You know something?" he asked abruptly as they were leaving the theater.

"What?"

"I keep feeling that we're off in the boonies somewhere and there's a war going on just over the hill. I keep feeling what we're getting hit by is wild shots from a cross fire going on just out of our line of sight."

"I guess you did see some of that movie after all," said Mattie dryly. "Nice image, but what does all that mean?"

"I think Jace is putting the move on Len," Bob said and Mattie turned and stared at him.

"What are you talking about?"

"I never could understand Len getting so hot under the collar about us working so close to the lab—unless it was because it *is* us. You heard him. 'Your good buddy,' he said. Maybe he took a swipe at us just because we *are* Jace's friends. And the more pressure Jace puts on, the more Len comes down on us. Only question is what's Jace doing to get him so riled?"

"That's pure speculation," Mattie murmured. But her heart thudded sharply in her breast.

He looked at her gravely. "I can't see Jace just walking out, Mattie. Not him. He's put roots down here. He's made a life. Maybe not the one he wants, but any life's hard to walk away from, specially when it's got a lot in it worth keeping."

It was a hope. And she clung to it.

Howard Lenkes, their lawyer, called early the next morning just as they were setting out to the barge.

"Just wanted to remind you the hearing date for Daviot's injunction is set for Friday," he said. "Will you have the barge up by then?"

"No chance," said Bob.

"Did you know that a couple of their top men are coming down? Inspection tour of the site, they say." He paused. "They'll be around Friday."

Bob grinned ruefully. "Len finally booted their legal machinery into motion, huh? How do you feel about going up against some really high-powered lawyers, Howie?"

"We'll win," said Howard confidently. But they had reservations. Anything could happen in court.

They tried to hurry the work, but there was a limit to how fast human bodies and metal torches could cut through heavy bulkheads underwater. Thursday evening they still had a long way to go.

Howard called late that night when they were all sitting glumly around, passing the bottle and feeling as if they should be holding a wake.

"The hearing's off," he said. "Canceled. Complaint's been withdrawn."

Bob yelped in triumph. "You're kidding! What did you do, put a hex on Daviot?"

"Wish I could take the credit, but I didn't do a thing." Howard sounded both puzzled and irritated. "Complaint's dropped; no explanation; that's it."

"Hell," Gramps said as they sat around the kitchen table, excitedly discussing it. "Len's decided to go the baseball-bat route."

"Good old Lemme-think-about-it Len?" Bob protested. "No way."

"Maybe we should put a watch on the platform. I wouldn't like to come back one morning and find she's just kinda slipped her anchor accidental-like during the night, and those pipes and cables we bust our backs putting in between her and the barge got all torn out."

"It's the weather that could do it, not Len," said Bob worriedly. The barometer was falling steadily and small craft advisories were out.

There was a great deal of activity going on at the Key Blanca site the next day when they checked it through the binoculars, but none of it seemed aimed at them. In fact, toward afternoon, the site broke out the two red pennants of a gale warning in case they were not aware of it.

But they already knew. They had been watching the squall line come steadily toward them for over an hour, a wall stretching for miles. The sky appeared bruised, livid with purpling cloud. Sections of the cloud wall glowed ominously from time to time from internal lightning, an irregular, recurrent pulse of pallid light.

Bob discontinued diving for the day.

"Go back home," he called to Tom Atkins and his crew aboard the other workboat.

"What about you?" Tom called back. Sounds were carrying sharply as the cloud ceiling thickened and lowered. The clang of a bell on the Key Blanca site came to them clear and penetrating.

"We're staying to keep an eye on the rig."

Tom pointed at the site where the square red flag with its black center of a storm warning had replaced the pennants. They could hear the storm now, a continuous growling mutter of thunder.

"It's going to be a real bad one, Bob!"

Bob looked around at the others. Everyone shook their heads.

"We'll ride it out. The rig's too important to lose."

Tom made a whirling motion of his forefinger at his temple, grinning. "Okay. See you later."

They watched him swing the *Maid* away through the whitecaps. The wind was rising, flinging spray at their faces, and the sea was beginning to heap up under the boats, lifting and dropping, lifting and dropping.

"Maybe we should make for harbor," Bob muttered, watching the squall line sweep rapidly toward them.

"And lose the rig?" Gramps demanded.

White foam was beginning to blow in long streaks from the breaking waves. They lashed down everything that could be lashed down, stowed everything else in the lockers and hold. The equipment on the rig was lashed but at risk, as was the whole platform. But there was no way to dismantle all the ties that connected it to the barge below in the time left to them.

"Mattie, can the *Marilee* ride it out?" Bob called.

Mattie waved jauntily from behind the wheel. "Sure. It's the rig I'm worried about."

The platform was plunging badly as the sea began to roll, jerking at the *Marilee* with every pitch.

"Maybe we should stand away from it," Bob muttered.

Mattie shook her head. "Don't worry. We'll be able to hold it if it slips its anchors. There's a lot of equipment on it, Bob."

"I know."

The first lash of the storm hit them just as dusk settled. Blackness fell like a curtain. The lights of the site vanished; only the two vertical red eyes of the storm-warning signal remained fitfully visible through the flung spray and the driving rain. Rain fell in a frenzy of sound; wind howled at them; thunder muttered continually, cracked like the breaking of gigantic tree limbs in sudden rips of lightning. The *Marilee* shuddered and complained under the lash of wind and water, tilting wildly on the waves.

Sam and Gramps huddled into the bridge with Mattie to snatch a cup of coffee. Bob stayed outside, watching the rig.

"Go below and get dry, Gramps," Mattie suggested. They were all shivering, pants soaked, arms wet to the shoulder where the wind drove rain up the arms of their slickers.

Gramps shook his head. "I'm staying as long as you are, girl. The animals may have taken over the zoo, but I'm still boss here."

Sam grinned at him. "It's time the young ones took over, Gramps. And they're doing a good job of it."

"Yeah, yeah, but I'm not ready for pasture yet," he growled and Mattie smiled at him.

"Not for a long time yet, Gramps."

"Mattie, listen," Sam said sharply, head tilted to the radio, which, as always when not in use, was tuned to the emergency channel. "Someone's in trouble."

It was not the Mayday emergency call, only the urgency signal, but that could be bad enough. They bent over the radio, straining to hear the words through the static crashes caused by the lightning.

"Sam, can you make it out?"

Sam was listening intently. "It's Len Daviot's *Princess*."

"The big yacht?" Gramps exclaimed, amazed. "What's he doing out on a night like this? He's a fair-weather sailor."

"Anyone hear him yet, Sam?" Mattie asked sharply.

"Got it!" He changed frequencies. "Chuck Fenton's cruiser, *Infinity's End* answered her. *Infinity*'s a lot closer than we are, Mattie."

"Good." If she had not been, they would have had to abandon the rig if Len was in real trouble.

They caught the yacht's position through crackles of static. *Infinity* was talking to her, telling her what to do as the cruiser worked her way slowly toward her.

"Daviot's turning west," Sam said sharply. "*Infinity*'s trying to tell him not to."

"West! Why?"

"I guess at that position he can see Key Mara, wants to make shore." He leaned out of the bridge, called, "Bob!"

"There are reefs all along there," Gramps muttered. "What the hell is that fool trying to do?"

"There's a channel through. Maybe he thinks he can make it."

"Hell, *I* couldn't make it."

Bob arrived, leaning through the door. "What's going on?"

Sam filled him in in a low-voiced mutter while they strained to hear through the static crashes. *Infinity* was pleading with the yacht to turn north.

"That bullheaded Daviot," Gramps muttered. "Wouldn't you know the one time he decides to stick his neck out it's the wrong time?"

Then there was only *Infinity* talking.

"What's going on; what's going on?" Gramps asked in a fever of impatience.

"She's hung up on the reef!" Sam exclaimed.

A new voice was coming over the radio, unmistakable even through the crashes of static. Jace's voice, crisp and exasperated, giving out position and status.

Mattie's head came up sharply. Her gaze and Bob's locked.

"Bob, cut the lines."

Bob nodded and went without a word.

"Mattie, *Infinity*'s closer," Gramps protested.

Sam went after Bob.

"Mattie, those reefs in this tub!"

Mattie was not listening. Gramps looked out of the bridge. Bob had already cast off the lines to the platform, leaving it to its own devices, was running to help Sam weigh anchor.

"You're all crazy," said Gramps, but he was grinning.

The *Marilee* was slow but she was steady. She plowed her way doggedly through the storm to Mara, rolling like a pig in the troughs but undeterred by the heavy seas crashing over her.

"There!" shouted Bob at the white shape barely glimpsed through the blackness and the waves.

The yacht had hung herself up solidly on the reef. They could not see whether she had holed herself, but from the angle she lay on the reef she was in no immediate danger of sinking.

Infinity had already reached her, but *Infinity* was a small craft and was having trouble holding her position what with the reef and the battering waves. Even so she had managed to get one man off and was trying for another. There were four left and one of them was lying injured on the yacht's deck.

Chuck Fenton, *Infinity*'s captain, raised an arm in relief as the *Marilee* beat her way toward them.

"I'll take it, Mattie," said Gramps and Mattie nodded, turned the wheel over to him and went to help Sam and Bob.

Gramps was a past master at this. He put the *Marilee* neatly alongside the yacht, held her there. *Infinity* had backed off, giving them clearance.

Two of the men stranded on the yacht were strangers, one green with seasickness and fumbling at the ropes they threw him, the other reasonably competent. The injured man was Len. The fourth was Jace.

Mattie, leaning over the side, saw the white flash of his grin as he looked up and saw her.

"Should have known it would be you!" he called, his voice barely audible over the yell of the wind, and she saw with exasperation that he was laughing. His face was vivid and vital with energy and enjoyment.

"Take Len first," he called, catching the ropes they threw him.

Len was already lashed into a sling. Jace and one of the strangers got the ropes hooked to him, braced him to keep him from slamming into *Marilee*'s side as Bob and Sam hauled him aboard. Bending far over to help the third man struggle over *Marilee*'s rail, Mattie saw Jace lean perilously over the yacht's side to make sure Bob and Sam had a good grip on Len. She cursed under her breath, dragged her man aboard and shoved him toward one of the lifelines strung along *Marilee*'s deck. Sick and shaking, he got a death grip on a line and satisfied as to his safety, she stumbled back to the side, staggering in the driving rain and the wash of water sweeping *Marilee*'s deck.

Bob and Sam had hauled Len aboard and Sam was reaching for the other man. Mattie could see Jace shouting instructions to him. She could not hear him over the wind but she knew he was telling the man to wait until the *Marilee* rolled toward them before jumping. His face was hard with concentration, but his mouth was smiling, and the eyes slitted against the driving rain and spray were alight with enjoyment. This was the whole man, assured and authoritative, motor turned full on, alive as she had never seen him before.

His eyes met hers as the *Marilee* rolled.

"Come on, damn you!" she shouted and he jumped.

Their hands locked and she threw her weight backward. A wave swept the *Marilee*. For a second there was a tearing weight on her right hand, then his free hand gripped her shoulder, her arm was around his waist, dragging him upward. Then they were sliding flat on their backs across the deck as the *Marilee* rolled away.

Another wave swept the deck, but this time Jace had his outstretched foot against a hatch, his free hand on a lifeline, and was holding them where they were. The wave swept over them, dragging at them. They came out of it, shaking their heads to clear the water from their eyes, half sitting, half lying on the deck, holding tightly to each other.

His head was in the curve of her shoulder. He turned it to look at her and that vibrant face was inches from hers, vivid and exhilarated, lips parted on a gust of fierce, bright laughter.

"You're a long way from home," he said.

"Damn you, Wyatt!" she spluttered, incoherent with rage and a crazy, helpless joy.

He kissed her, fast and hard, and she felt his laughter, with his kiss, run through her like wildfire.

Then the next wave crashed over them, swamping them.

"Water and you don't mix," he said when they could breathe again. "We'll attract a lightning stroke next. I'll talk to you on dry land, Mattie."

She pushed him away furiously and scrambled to her feet.

"*If* I let you, you'd better have plenty to say, Jace Wyatt!"

She stalked away, furious that her exit was somewhat marred by the pitching of the boat, aware of him laughing behind her as he got to his feet.

This was a man she didn't know—confident, assured, lighthearted, wickedly teasing.

"I'll take it!" she snapped as she flung into the bridge.

"Everyone off?" Gramps handed over the wheel. "Jace all right?"

"Too damn all right," she said between her teeth and Gramps stared at her in astonishment.

"Uh, I'd better take care of those guys. That'll free up the boys to help you."

"Right."

She eased the *Marilee* away from the reef, concentrating fiercely on that to quell the conflicting impulses of anger and confusion and joy that swept her. Instinctively she headed for Key Vaca and home. *Infinity* was already on her way, making for the same destination.

Bob came up a while later to report that Len had a slight concussion which should be checked out at the hospital, but seemed to be okay. The other two men were no more than bruised and battered and extremely seasick. They were the higher-ups Howard had mentioned, being given a tour of the area, Bob said with much amusement.

"And then there's Jace," she murmured.

Bob looked at her warily. "Yeah."

"He just came along for the ride, I suppose."

"That's what he says," he agreed and grinned involuntarily.

"Do me a favor," Mattie said sweetly and he gave her a nervous glance. "When we get home, go lock Gramps in the head for a couple of hours."

"Sam and I already agreed to do just that thing," said Bob and laughed.

With Gramps and the two passengers out of the way below, the four of them made one sweetly operating team. They got the *Marilee* docked in no time at all, and

Sam and Bob slung out the gangway and ran to help *Infinity*.

Mattie was just turning to leave the bridge when Jace's bulk blocked the doorway.

"I want to talk to you." His head was tilted back, his jaw aggressively outthrust. "Will you let me?"

She drew a brief, shuddering breath. "Do I have a choice?"

He looked at her unsmilingly, all laughter gone, his eyes still and vulnerable.

"Yes," he said simply and all the anger ran out of her.

"Why couldn't you have said no?" she wailed. "Then I could simply have decked you."

Involuntarily he smiled. "You'd have tried, wouldn't you, all one-hundred-odd pounds of you."

"Damn right."

"Will you come?"

"Yes. Where?"

He looked at the main house where the lights had already gone on. They both visualized the bustle that would take up the next couple of hours, the lack of privacy.

"The beachhouse."

She nodded. His hand came lightly under her elbow, steadying her against the lash of the rain; his body curved to shield her from the worst buffets of the wind. She had missed that unconscious cherishing of his and it caught at her throat so that she wanted to turn right there and lean into him and feel his warmth all around her.

He reached past her to open the door of the beachhouse, shut it behind them, leaning his shoulder against the door to close it against the blast of the wind. Mattie went on into the living room and turned to face him.

He lit the light switch and they both blinked in the sudden blaze of light and for a moment were both still, regarding each other warily.

Then Jace moved, stripping off his slicker. "I'll light a fire."

He crossed the room, wiping water from his face with the palm of his hand.

"There are towels in the bathroom," she said and dropped her slicker on top of his on the floor and went to get them.

He had the fire going when she came back, and swung around on one knee to catch the towel she tossed him.

She turned away from him, suddenly shy, dried herself quickly, then finger combed her damp hair straight back from her face.

"Are you angry?" he asked, still one one knee, looking up at her. He had made no effort to dry himself, simply knelt there, watching her every move with intent eyes.

"No."

"You have reason to be," he said quietly.

Her gaze lifted helplessly to his. "I never could stay angry with you."

He made an abrupt movement toward her, then checked himself sharply.

She turned to him as he stood up, but he was only crossing to the liquor cabinet, drying his face and hair roughly as he went. He threw the towel down, poured them both a brandy, held a glass out to her.

She came and took it and his fingers closed over hers, holding her where she was.

"You've forgiven me, haven't you?" he said in wonder. "Without explanations, without question. You'd let me walk back into your life just like that."

"I told you once," she said simply, "you could always walk back."

He bent suddenly and kissed her fingers.

"I love you," he said.

Her gaze shot to his face, her eyes wide and incredulous.

"I thought that was a word you didn't use," she whispered. "All those words—love and loyalty and forever—all of them, you didn't believe in them."

"You changed that," he said and her gaze searched his face, finding it tense and strained. "Do you remember I once said to you if I had one thing I could believe in, then I could believe in all the rest? And you said I could try believing in you."

She nodded. "And you said you couldn't."

"I could. I did."

If his hands had not been cupping hers around the brandy glass, she would have dropped it.

"And then everything else became possible," he said.

"I don't understand," she whispered.

He let her go and moved away across the room, pacing it. She put the glass down untouched, and leaned against the wall beside the liquor cabinet, watching him.

"It took me just two weeks to realize that I couldn't make it without you, Mattie. When I came here, there was an emptiness in me, a hole exactly your size and shape. You filled it; you made me whole. I thought I could go back to the way it was before. But I couldn't. Even for your sake I couldn't."

He turned and looked at her.

"I could never give Ellie the one thing she wanted: I couldn't leave the sea for her. And now I couldn't give you the things you wanted—permanence, stability, a life with which we could both be content."

"That didn't matter to me, Jace."

"I didn't want any more sacrifices! Sacrifice is not something on which to build any kind of life! We both had to gain, not one at the expense of the other. We had to meet as equals on equal ground. I couldn't see any way that could happen. So I left."

She was silent, watching him, knowing he was not finished.

"Instead of cursing the darkness you light a candle, right? It took me a long time to realize that if I wanted things to be different I had to go and make them different. It took you to make me realize I could make a difference."

"I don't understand."

"What we needed was a world that would let me do something that could be really useful and one that would also let you stay in the Keys. Because you couldn't be happy without the *Queen* and the charters any more than I could be with just the salvage. But there wasn't one. So I thought that was it. Until I realized that I could make one."

She made a tiny gesture of bewilderment and he smiled faintly.

"The lab, Mattie. You want permanence, stability? That lab's going to operate for decades. They'll need a technical director even after the construction's complete, even more once the scientists move in and air, life-support, and submersible travel between lab and surface become essential."

Her lips parted in swift understanding and involuntary laughter. "Bob kept saying it was you giving poor Len all that trouble!"

"All Len could see was that his control might be weakened. He couldn't appreciate that with someone with technical knowledge backing up his decisions things would move faster and his position would only be strengthened. It took me a while to convince him I wasn't after his job."

"He said you went over his head to the board. He was furious."

Jace smiled crookedly. "One thing I do know is how to go through channels. I was careful not to make him look bad. He isn't holding any grudges, was reconciled enough to invite me along on this cruise."

"You made him drop that injunction."

He nodded. "It took two months to convince him, to convince the board. But it worked. All it was, Mattie, was a hope, a promise that could have been empty. I could build nothing on that. But now it's worked and now I can."

A little silence fell. He was standing with his hands in his pockets, his head down and his eyes watching her with that up-from-under cat stare that was so demanding.

"So," she murmured. "What now?"

"Now I want us to get married."

"Ah," she said and leaned back against the wall, her eyes languid and faintly mocking. "I'll have to think about that."

He began to smile. "You have reservations?"

"I think I want to be courted. The last time I did all the chasing."

"That can be arranged. About forty or fifty years worth. After the wedding of course."

She looked at him provocatively, smiling. "Maybe I'd like to play the field awhile."

"You've had two months to do that. You're not going to get another chance. From now on I'm going to be everywhere you turn. I'm going to follow you around, and if you even look sideways at another man I'm going to take him out."

"You could, couldn't you?" she murmured. His eyes were alight with dark laughter and complete assurance, and an irrepressible bubble of answering laughter and delight was beginning to rise in her, fizz in her blood like bubbles in champagne.

"You know I can."

He came suddenly across the room toward her and her breath caught in her throat and she laughed up at him as his hands flattened on the wall on either side of her.

"This is your new game plan, is it?" she asked. "Forcing things to be the way you want them?"

"That's exactly right."

She pressed herself flatter against the wall. He was not touching her, but she could feel the warmth of his body, his breath against her mouth. His face filled her vision. She was intensely aware of that supple, powerful body inches from hers, of the urgent imperative heat between them that had not ceased with separation.

"All those weeks away from you, Mattie," he whispered, echoing her thought the way they always could with each other. "And every time I closed my eyes I could *feel* you against me; I could feel you."

"Don't," she whispered, but her breath shook in her mouth and her whole body was melting, slumping against the wall as her bones turned to water.

His lips were a fraction of an inch from her skin, moving tantalizingly over her face without touching her, making her unbearably aware of the seductive cave of his open mouth. They knew each other too well, were so sensitized to each other that he could seduce her with just his breath on her face and the warmth of his body and the nearness of him. And that was exactly what he was doing—seducing her, deliberately, expertly, dark eyes smiling and sensual.

"I love you, Mattie," he said a fraction of an inch from her mouth and her hands came up to cling drowningly to the broad wrists on either side of her head.

"That's not fair."

His body brushed lightly against hers and only her hands clenched on his wrists kept her from going straight down to the ground under the shock of pure fire that shot through her.

"Damn it, Jace," she mumbled, breathless and laughing, and he leaned suddenly full on her, chest and flat stomach and taut hips pressing her against the wall, body moving in supple stretches against her, deliberately inflaming her.

"Mattie, one word . . ."

"Yes," she whispered helplessly.

"Yes what?"

Her arms came fiercely up around him.

"Yes, I love you and yes, I'll marry you and yes, I swear I'll kill you if you ever do this to me again!"

His mouth came down on hers, hard. She drowned in him.

He was holding her crushed so tightly against him that she could not breathe, but she didn't need breath. Teetering on tiptoe, bent backward over the steel bar of his arm, she had no balance, but she didn't need balance. She needed only this, his mouth on hers, his body insistent against hers, all the solid sensual reality of him in her arms.

She couldn't get close enough, couldn't hold him tightly enough. She strained against him, kissing his eyes and his throat and the crease between his brows, everywhere she could reach, her arms fast about him.

He made an odd painful sound in his throat.

"Oh, how I've wanted you," he said and his voice was a rasp in his throat, suffocated and intense. "I've been dying for you every second of every unendurable day for the past two months."

"I'm glad," she said fiercely. "I'm glad. That makes us even."

He picked her up suddenly and carried her to the bedroom and tumbled her gently on the bed, then was beside her, his weight coming briefly upon her as he leaned over her to switch on the one lamp beside the bed. By that time her arms were around him and her mouth was sliding down the lovely long tendon at the side of his neck.

He caught her head and held it still, looking down at her with intent brooding wonder as if surprised to see her there. His hands stroked her face; his bent head and arms and the splay of his shoulders formed a warm sweet protective wall around her head. His face was tight with passion, but his eyes were open and clear. There were no shadows in them any more, no shadows at all, only a love and delight so intense and helpless that her heart clenched painfully within her breast and she looked at him with drowning tenderness.

"Never stop looking at me like that," he muttered. "You're the only woman who has ever made my mouth go dry just thinking about her, but I've needed that look more than I've needed breath."

"I wouldn't know how to stop," she said simply.

He kissed her with sudden ravenous hunger. His hands caught her clammy sweater, dragged it up over her head. She was already tearing at his. Together they struggled out of the damp wool, fell back on the bed, gasping a little at the shock of racking satisfaction at the rub of skin against skin, that imperative flare of blood heat.

His hands and his mouth slid over her shoulders and breasts and rib cage, igniting her until she writhed mindlessly under him, aware of nothing but those intense, unbearably knowledgeable caresses, whispering crazy incoherent words, her own hands rediscovering the marvelous territory of his body, pushing demandingly down under the belt of his jeans so that he shuddered and lurched involuntarily against her.

"Oh, no," he muttered. "No. I've been wanting this too long to let it be over so soon."

"But I want you now," she growled and bit him deliberately hard and felt his rib cage jolt against hers with answering laughter.

In fierce half-laughing impatience they wrestled out of the rest of their clothes, flinging them away, coming back breathless and no longer laughing into each other's arms, legs tangling, falling on each other famished and urgent.

She had not thought it possible it could ever be better than it was before, but this was better; this was unbearably perfect, with his lips muttering crazy love words and his hands cherishing her and his eyes watching her with helpless wondering delight while the deep slow powerful thrusts of his body stretched her on a rack of unendurable pleasure.

She raked his flat stomach with her nails and her body clenched on him, and he panted and his eyes went blind and his body slammed against hers, all control lost, and the storm swept them over the edge into mindless, blinding ecstasy.

She must have slept because the next thing she knew she was lying on her side, pressed to the length of him, her head in the curve of his shoulder, his thigh between hers and his free hand tracing lightly over the contours of her face and body, a drifting repetitive lingering touch.

"How long have you been awake?" she murmured, rubbing her face against his shoulder.

"I don't know. Hours, I think." He bent and kissed her slowly. "Do you have any idea of what you've done for me, Mattie?"

She stroked his face tenderly. "I'm not sure."

"You've given me back myself. Before I came here the world was all in shades of gray. You've given me back color. You've given me back life and hope and belief. I love you. I love you," he said slowly and with emphasis. "Do you know what it means to be able to say that again?"

"I know what it means to hear it," she whispered and his arms tightened around her.

"I'm going to love you forever, Mattie. I'm never going to stop loving you. That's an article of faith. There." He grinned suddenly at her. "I've used all the words, Mattie, every single one, and I mean them. How do you like that?''

"I like it fine," she said and hugged him.

She had never expected to see him this way, carefree and vibrant and very young with that charming, cocky triumph. It was delightful.

"So do I. I could knock down mountains; you know that? I could go out and battle giants. Want me to prove it? I feel like I could do anything.''

She was laughing. "Why not? You've already conquered reality, haven't you?''

"A real Eden in the real world." He grinned down at her. "How's that for making a difference?''

"Not bad," she murmured. "It makes me nervous wondering what you might take on next.''

"What we might take on," he corrected, smiling. Then his arms pulled her closer. "We made it, Mattie. I never thought we would. We've got it all now. Everything we want.''

She drew him down to her. "Everything I want? Oh, yes, Jace. Right here. Right here in my arms.''

*   *   *   *   *

 *Silhouette Desire* ®

COMING
NEXT MONTH

#517 BEGINNER'S LUCK—Dixie Browning
Meet September's *Man of the Month*, Clement Barto. Mating habits:
unexplored. Women scared him speechless—literally. But with a little
beginner's luck, Clem was about to discover something called love....

#518 THE IDEAL MAN—Naomi Horton
Corporate headhunter Dani Ross had to find the right man for a client—
but the job title was "Husband." When she met rancher Jake Montana
she knew he was ideal—for her!

#519 ADAM'S WAY—Cathie Linz
Business efficiency expert Julia Trent insisted on a purely professional
relationship with problem-solver Adam MacKenzie. But he was
determined to make her see things Adam's way.

#520 ONCE IN LOVE WITH JESSIE—Sally Goldenbaum
Who says opposites don't attract? Confirmed bachelor Matt Ridgefield
had been content with his solitary life-style before carefree, spirited Jessie
Sager had come along. The professor had a lot to learn!

#521 ONE TOUCH OF MOONDUST—Sherryl Woods
Paul Reed was the most *romantic* man Gabrielle Clayton had ever met. H
was also her new roommate—and suddenly practical Gaby was dreaming
of moonlight and magic.

#522 A LIVING LEGEND—Nancy Martin
Hot on the trail of the scoop of the century, Catty Sinclair found only
gruff recluse Seth Bernstein. What *was* this gorgeous man doing in the
middle of nowhere...?

AVAILABLE NOW:

Silhouette Special Edition

presents

★ LOVE AND GLORY ★

from
Lindsay McKenna

Introducing a gripping new series celebrating our men—and women—in uniform. Meet the Trayherns, a military family as proud and colorful as the American flag, a family fighting the shadow of dishonor, a family determined to triumph—with **LOVE AND GLORY!**

June: A QUESTION OF HONOR (SE #529) leads the fast-paced excitement. When Coast Guard officer Noah Trayhern offers Kit Anderson a safe house, he unwittingly endangers his own guarded emotions.

July: NO SURRENDER (SE #535) Navy pilot Alyssa Trayhern's assignment with arrogant jet jockey Clay Cantrell threatens her career—and her heart—with a crash landing!

August: RETURN OF A HERO (SE #541) Strike up the band to welcome home a man whose top-secret reappearance will make headline news . . . with a delicate, daring woman by his side.

If you missed any of the LOVE AND GLORY titles send your name, address and zip or postal code, along with a check or money order for $2.95 for each book ordered, plus 75¢ postage and handling, payable to Silhouette Reader Service to:

In Canada
P.O. Box 609
Fort Erie, Ontario
L2A 5X3

In USA
901 Furhmann Blvd.
P.O. Box 1396
Buffalo, NY 14269-1396

Please specify book title with your order.

LG-1A

Silhouette Intimate Moments®

AWARD OF EXCELLENCE

NORA ROBERTS
brings you the first
Award of Excellence title
Gabriel's Angel
coming in August from
Silhouette Intimate Moments

They were on a collision course with love....

*Laura Malone was alone, scared—and pregnant. She was running
for the sake of her child. Gabriel Bradley had his own problems.
He had neither the need nor the inclination to get involved in
someone else's.*

*But Laura was like no other woman... and she needed him. Soon
Gabe was willing to risk all for the heaven of her arms.*

The Award of Excellence is given to one specially selected title per
month. Look for the second Award of Excellence title, coming out in
September from Silhouette Romance—**SUTTON'S WAY**
by Diana Palmer

Im 300-1

Silhouette Romance®

SUTTON'S WAY
by Diana Palmer

In Diana Palmer's bestselling Long, Tall Texans trilogy, you had a mesmerizing glimpse of Quinn Sutton—a mean, lean Wyoming wildcat of a man with a disposition to match.

Now, in September, Quinn's back with a story of his own. Set in the Wyoming wilderness, he learns a few things about women from snowbound beauty Amanda Callaway—and a lot more about love.

He's a Texan at heart . . . who soon has a Wyoming wedding in mind!

Spend September discovering *Sutton's Way* #670 . . . only in Silhouette Romance.

RS670-1

Silhouette Romance®

JOIN TOP-SELLING AUTHOR
EMILIE RICHARDS
FOR A SPECIAL ANNIVERSARY

Only in September, and only in Silhouette Romance, we are bringing you Emilie's twentieth Silhouette novel, *Island Glory* (SR #675).

Island Glory brings back Glory Kalia, who made her first—and very memorable—appearance in *Aloha Always* (SR #520). Now she's here with a story—and a hero—of her own. Thrill to warm tropical nights with Glory and Jared Farrell, a man who doesn't want to give any woman his heart but quickly learns that, with Glory, he has no choice.

Join Silhouette Romance for September and experience a taste of *Island Glory*.

RS675-1